DATE DUE

AUG 28 2001	
AUG 29 2001	
SEP 19 2001	
NOV 30 2001	

RIDE THE RED TRAIL

A Western Trio

Other Five Star Titles
by Lewis B. Patten:

Tincup in the Storm Country
Trail to Vicksburg
Death Rides the Denver Stage
The Woman at Ox-Yoke

RIDE THE RED TRAIL

A Western Trio

LEWIS B. PATTEN

Five Star • Waterville, Maine

Five Star First Edition Western Series.

Published in 2001 in conjunction with
Golden West Literary Agency.

Set in 11 pt. Plantin by Al Chase.

Printed in the United States on permanent paper.

Library of Congress Cataloging-in-Publication Data

Patten, Lewis B.
Ride the red trail : a Western trio / by Lewis B. Patten. —1st ed.
p. cm.
Contents: Summer kill—Ride the red trail—Rustler's run.
ISBN 0-7862-2764-8 (hc : alk. paper)
1. Western stories. I. Title.
PS3566.A79 R56 2001

2001023678

TABLE OF CONTENTS

Summer Kill

It was difficult in the early 1950s for a new Western author to sell a book-length novel to a hardcover publisher. Those publishers that had Western fiction lines—principally Doubleday, Macmillan, and Dutton—had a group of established authors writing books for their lists. For Lewis B. Patten, the easier route to follow was the one he pursued: writing for the Western fiction magazine market. It wouldn't be until 1952 that Patten was able to sell a Western novel, and in that case it was an original paperback, MASSACRE AT WHITE RIVER, published as one half of a double-action Western book by Ace Publishing. Patten was paid less than a thousand dollars for that sale, while the magazines allowed him to maintain a steadier income. "Summer Kill" first appeared in *Triple Western* (10/53), a bimonthly magazine published by Standard Magazines that featured three short novels in every issue, with usually one of them being a reprint. During the war years Patten had worked as a senior auditor for the State of Colorado in the Department of Revenue, a background that may well have influenced the writing of this story.

I

Old Ben Malloy stepped out onto the long verandah. A breeze, carrying the rich smell of drying hay, stirred his long, thinning gray hair, cooled his heated face. His brows spread away from his sharp, hooked nose like the wings of a soaring hawk. His pale lips were thin-drawn against his yellowed teeth. His hands were shaking with rage. Huge disgust welled up within him. Damn a man that couldn't keep his hands out of someone else's pockets!

Anger had brought words from his mouth back there that he didn't mean, that should never have been said. He'd threatened Hirons with prison, for one thing. Hell, he wouldn't put any man behind bars, not for a simple act of stealing, at least.

He stepped down off the verandah, stiff with increased rage, yet active and sure in spite of the weakness and dizziness that came these days whenever anger stirred him. Because he had always faced trouble this way, he now headed for the big corral where half a dozen horses drowsed in the early darkness. With a sure hand, he roped his big dappled gray out of the bunch. The horse stood quietly as Ben Malloy threw up the saddle and cinched it down, and remained so while the old man mounted. He took the trail that wound upward onto the knoll behind the house with only the twitch of the reins to start him.

The old man scowled. His hand, holding the reins, was thin and bony, covered with freckled skin that was dry and smooth, like paper. His chin sunk down upon his chest, and he let the gray pick his own path. The moon, butter-yellow, poked its broad top rim above the horizon, bathing the wide valley with its long-shadowed glow.

Now that it was too late, Ben guessed he could see a lot of mistakes he had made along the years. There were his two boys, Phil and Ed, men now, Ben realized with a touch of reluctant surprise. For a long time, Ben had felt a sense of inadequacy and failure where the boys were concerned. A man got used to brushing his sons aside as they grew because he could do things that needed doing so much better himself. He had failed to place in their proper relationship of importance those things that needed doing, now long forgotten, and the growth of competence in his maturing sons. After half a dozen years of being pushed aside, he guessed he couldn't blame them much for the to-hell-with-it attitude they had developed. Ed would never have made a bookkeeper and business manager, anyway, Ben realized, but Phil might have. He probably would not have been as efficient as Lenny Hirons, but at least he'd have been honest.

At the top of the knoll, the old man reined up and stared down at the sprawling collection of buildings. Then, twitching the reins again, he moved west down the slope, passing from bright moonlight into dark, concealing shadow. He smiled wryly as he realized which trail the horse was taking tonight. It was as if the animal, through long association with the old man, knew his mind, thereby knowing which of the three trails he was expected to take.

There was the troubled trail that old Ben rode when he was angry or troubled and that always ended in the pile of loosely strewn boulders on the top of Old Baldy at the west end of the park. Another trail entirely did he take when he was pleased or extraordinarily happy about something. Still a third trail did he follow when he was lonely and blue, and this one always led him to the grave of his wife, eastward at the site of their first cabin, clear off the Gunsight Grant entirely.

Old Ben, a creature of strong habit, was as predictable as the regular succession of the seasons. He was predictable to all who knew him—even to Lenny Hirons. After old Ben had left, Hirons sat at his desk in the ranch office, books and ledgers piled before him, and wiped the beaded sweat from his pale and worried brow. He hadn't thought the old man was sharp enough to spot his defalcations; he hadn't thought the old man knew what he was doing when he looked at the books. Regularly old Ben perused Lenny's records, but Lenny had supposed he did that simply to make a show of his awareness of what was going on. Lenny had a sort of contempt for the old man, the amused contempt of youth for age, of the cursorily educated for the unlettered.

Lenny was thin, wiry, and bespectacled. He looked older than he was. He was twenty-eight. His skin contrasted sharply in color to the weathered complexions of Gunsight Grant's ranch hands, for Lenny did not like the sun or the open air. He liked his dry and dusty office, his heavy ledgers and neat files. He liked money, too, not so much for the money itself, or the things it could buy, but for the security it guaranteed.

His expression was panicky as he stood up. His security was threatened now. He looked ahead at the bleak years, behind bars at the territorial prison. He looked at his hands. They had begun to shake violently with the idea that had begun to grow in his mind. He began to sweat even more profusely. He sat down again at the desk and riffled nervously through the pages of one of the ledgers. At last his mouth firmed out. He stood up, put on his derby hat and coat. From the rack of antlers over the fireplace, he took down a Winchester carbine. He poked a handful of shells into its loading gate. Then he went out onto the verandah and stared at the yard, bright-washed with summer moonlight.

He knew old Ben's habits, knew about his troubled trail, knew as well about the others. Gunsight's ranch hands frequently joked affectionately about old Ben's three trails. And Old Baldy was plainly visible in the distance from the knoll in back of the house, visible even tonight, because of the moon.

Lenny went down off the porch, and slid along in the shadow of the house. From there it was but a short ten feet to the dappled shade of the huge cottonwood. When he crossed from the cottonwood to the corral, he held the rifle pointed down against his leg so that it would not be visible to anyone who happened to see him. He hoped no one would. But it was a chance he had to take.

At the corral, he leaned the rifle against the poles while he caught and saddled a horse. Fifty yards away the bunkhouse door was open. Smoke drifting from it was visible in the beam of lamp glow that fell in a square on the ground before it. Luke Borden was playing his mandolin and singing. Lenny hoped the sound of Luke's nasal voice would cover the sound of his departure.

He went over the rest of Gunsight's complement in his mind. Both Ed and Phil Malloy were absent from Gunsight, and had been for several days. Probably in Fernándo, gambling or drinking. Swigert, the sour old cook, was washing dishes in the kitchen. Hirons wondered if Swigert could have heard old Ben shouting in the office. He didn't think he could. He recalled how difficult it was to hear what went on in the kitchen from the office door. A lamp burned upstairs in Sarah Montano's room. She was reading, Hirons supposed. She was always reading.

He began to be afraid. There were so damned many things

that could trip him up. If someone saw him leaving or returning, if Swigert had heard the quarrel, if someone missed him while he was gone. . . . He remembered suddenly that he had left the lamp burning in the office, but he knew he could not risk going back now.

He retrieved the rifle as he swung up into saddle. He rode at a walk, going away from yard and buildings until he hit the bed of Icewater Creek. He followed this until he could no longer hear Luke's singing. Then he climbed out and circled westward toward Old Baldy.

He was not overly familiar with the contour of the country. He did not need to be tonight. The rising moon, nearly full, illumined the low peak, made it stand out like a sentinel. For thirty minutes, Lenny headed a full ten degrees to the left of it. Then he pointed his horse at its southern foot. He knew old Ben would be riding slowly. He knew that he could reach the peak ahead of the old man easily.

Yet, as he rode, nervousness was on the increase in him. He did not think old Ben was wearing a gun, but he could not be sure. There had been too much poverty in Lenny's early life. There was too great a thirst in him for security for him to be handling another man's money. Poverty, and hunger, and an insatiable thirst for security—these were the things Lenny had lived with, these were the things that had shaped him. He admitted now that he hadn't played it too smart. Instead of manipulating the books as he could have done, he had simply pocketed certain ranch receipts and failed to enter them. In a few cases he had entered diminished amounts, and had kept the balance. He had not considered that the old man's memory might be unfailing.

Old Ben had missed the payment for two horses sold to a homesteader who was passing through. Going over the books then, he had missed other payments and had confronted

Lenny with his knowledge tonight. Lenny had nearly five thousand in gold hidden in his room. He was damned if he'd give it up. He was also damned if he'd go to jail for stealing it. This, then, was the answer. But as he approached the slope of Old Baldy, Lenny began to shiver. He rode halfway up the slope, screened in timber, and tied his horse to a tree at its upper fringe. Then, afoot and carrying the rifle, he continued upward toward the boulder-strewn top.

The top was a sort of flat park, no more than a quarter mile across. It was strewn with five-to-fifteen-foot boulders, as though eons ago, giants had played marbles here and had gone off and forgotten their game. Lenny stationed himself behind a rock that was but slightly shorter than himself, and sat down to wait. Gloomily his mind went backward as he sought to dredge up enough resentment, and enough self-justification, for the thing he was about to do.

Lenny's story was the story of a misfit in a land where most activity was of the physical variety. Marooned in Dodge City ten years before the death of both father and mother from smallpox, he had left his sister and little brother in the hands of a family there who offered to feed and clothe them in exchange for the sister's work, and had set out westward to seek his own fortune, good or bad. He had tried punching cows for a small outfit in Arizona, barely escaping from raiding Apaches with his life. From there he had gone to Tombstone. He guessed that in Tombstone had happened the thing that had so definitely marked him as a man not meant for physical pursuits. Just turned nineteen, he had taken to carrying a gun, as almost everyone did. He had taken to drinking occasionally, and to the two circumstances could be attributed his scarring experience. A quarrel, a challenge, a choice of backing down or getting killed. Lenny had backed down. He was not the first man who had backed away from certain death in a fight. But the scarring effect of the experience in Lenny's mind was terrible. In his own mind, he was plainly branded coward.

He had left Tombstone, of course. He had gone to Montana but, finding the winters more rigorous than he liked, drifted south again, through Wyoming, into Colorado, working along the way as clerk in a store, as bartender or swamper in saloons, even as a barber in a town that had none. He had been picked up by Ben Malloy in Fernándo, broke and hungry and down on his luck. Ever since he had kept books for Gunsight Grant.

Lenny straightened from his place behind the boulder. Below him, toward Gunsight, he heard the ring of a shod hoof against rock. He began to tremble uncontrollably. Blood drained out of his face, leaving it ghastly white. Ben Malloy had mentioned prison, had demanded restitution. Lenny tried to hold that in his mind, found that it steadied his hands.

He saw the old man coming upslope toward him a hundred yards away. In the bright moonlight, he could see that old Ben's head was sunk down onto his chest, almost as though he were asleep. Carefully, almost silently, Lenny levered a cartridge into the Winchester's firing chamber. He stood up carefully, keeping his body behind the boulder. He rested the rifle cautiously on the top of it. Moonlight struck his gunsights, illuminating them plainly enough for good shooting. Lenny drew a long breath. He drew a bead on the old man's chest. Before he could tremble, or change his mind, he squeezed off the trigger.

The roar of the Winchester was deafening in the utter quiet of the peak. The flash blinded Hirons. He jumped back and to one side, ready to run, wanting desperately to run. He could hear the sounds of the old man's retreating horse briefly, and then silence.

Blinded by the flash of the rifle, Lenny had not seen the old man fall. He was aware that he could not leave until he had made sure that the old man was dead, for if Ben Malloy had escaped, then Hirons had better mount up and leave the country as fast as a running horse could carry him.

He forced himself to turn, to scan the ground where the old man's horse had stood. There was a dark and low-lumped shape on the ground. It lay, unmoving and silent. Lenny levered another shell into the gun. Almost overpowering were his fear and his impulse to run. But he forced himself to approach the old man, rifle held tightly against his shoulder, pointing down at the old man on the ground.

This was the first time that Lenny had killed in his whole life. He muttered aloud: "I'm a coward, am I? And a thief? But even a coward can kill. Did you know that? Even a coward can kill!"

He poked Ben's body with the muzzle of the rifle. It twitched, the flesh nervously contracting even in death. Lenny's panicked finger tightened on the trigger. He knew where that bullet went. It went straight into the old man's chest cavity. Without waiting longer, Lenny turned and ran.

II

Gunsight Grant was a huge bowl, a park bounded on all four sides by towering, spruce-clad peaks. Containing over a hundred and sixty thousand acres, it was an original Spanish land grant. Ben Malloy had bought it from the descendants of the original grantees for a fraction of its value, only because he was not interested in minerals and offered to let the owner retain the mineral rights.

The Fernándo family moved from the sprawling ranch house to the edge of the park where Icewater Creek began its tumbling descent to the plains. There they struck placer gold in fabulous quantities and built a town that they named Fernándo. They lived now in solitary grandeur atop a low ridge before the town in a house that was a gingerbread monstrosity of three-storied stone.

Below, the town grew and brawled, killed and raped, howled and sweated. It had eight saloons, and one church that the Fernándos themselves had built and paid for. In addition to the saloons it had three general stores, five assay offices, and two livery barns. One hotel catered to the more substantial of Fernándo's citizens, and the other to the miners. Money poured, a golden stream into the Fernándo coffers, for from each claim located on Gunsight Grant they received twenty percent royalty.

In the Nugget Saloon, Ed Malloy tipped back his chair and held his cards close to his vest. He looked at the four other players. He grinned and said: "Fifty." He shoved three gold coins into the center of the table.

The man on his left tossed his cards disgustedly into the pot. "Pass."

Malloy's grin widened. He was a tall young man, not yet twenty-five. His grinning face showed the effects of liquor only in its heightened color and the added brightness of his eyes. His shoulders were broad without heaviness, his chest full without excessive thickness. He was dressed like a working 'puncher, and his broad-brimmed Stetson was pushed back on his head to reveal short black hair that tended to curl.

Juan Fernándo, second on his left, complained: "Ed, damn it, you've got too much luck tonight." He grinned, saying then regretfully: "I've got two nice pairs, but I've got to pass." He tossed in his cards.

Ed Malloy said humorously: "You should have kept those, Juan. Maybe they'd have beat me."

"Uhn-uh. I know you."

Ed squinted at Juan's brother Miguel. "Feel lucky?"

Miguel Fernándo was sheriff, but he was apologetic about the fact. Self-effacing and sometimes overly polite, he could nevertheless handle the tough mining town his family had created. He was of a size with Juan, was perhaps five years older. He was thirty-five. With hooded eyes he stared at Ed. He said: "Somebody's got to keep you honest, and Doc here has consigned his hand to the discard already." He cocked an inquiring eye at Doc Blanchard. "That right, Doc?"

Doc nodded. He tossed his cards onto the pile.

Miguel said: "I've got to see them, Ed."

Ed flipped his hand face down upon the table. He held four treys.

Miguel shrugged. "I knew you had 'em. There's a difference in your grin when you don't."

Ed mocked: "Why didn't you save your money then?"

Miguel shrugged. "What for? I wanted to see your hand." He tipped a brown bottle and filled his glass, passing the bottle to Ed.

Ed started to pour himself a drink, but suddenly stopped. He'd had the strangest feeling as he touched the bottle. He stood up abruptly, without quite knowing why he did. He was enjoying himself. He was winning. He liked the company of the Fernándos and of Doc Blanchard. He was even beginning to like the taciturn stranger who sat on his left. But suddenly he had no more stomach either for liquor or poker.

Juan asked: "What's the matter?"

Ed shrugged, scowling. "I guess I'm tired of playing." He raked his pile of gold coins into his hand and dropped them into his pocket.

Doc rose, yawning. "Guess I'll quit, too."

Ed asked: "What time is it, Doc?"

Blanchard fished for his watch, muttering. "Past midnight." He looked at the watch. "Ten minutes to one."

Ed took his cartridge belt and holstered gun from the chair back where he had hung it when he'd sat down to play. He buckled it about his middle. It occurred to him that he hadn't been home to Gunsight in nearly a week. He wondered how old Ben was making out. He said—"I'll give you a chance to get even next time I'm in town."—to all four men at once, and turned toward the door.

Cold night air was pleasant and stinging in his nostrils. The town of Fernándo on the Gunsight Grant was nestled at an elevation of nearly eight thousand feet. It was never really warm at night, not even in summer.

A drunken miner staggered against him, cursed him. Ed grinned and moved out of the man's way. The miner went on down the street. Ed stepped down into the street and angled across toward the livery barn where he kept his horse. He knew that Mike Donovan would be asleep. He wondered briefly why the hell he'd taken this sudden notion to go home. Everybody'd be asleep. He wouldn't see a soul until morning, anyway.

He hesitated for a moment in mid-street. Then resolutely he went on to the stable. He found his horse in its accustomed stall, saddled, and rode out.

At the edge of town, a hundred yards to the left of the road that led out to Gunsight Grant, a canvas-topped wagon was parked. Two mules were tied to a cottonwood close by. The embers of a fire glowed against the ground near the wagon. A clothesline had been strung between the two trees, and on the line hung a couple of woman's dresses, some underwear, boy-size, and a pair of woolen pants, also boy-size.

Ed lifted his horse to a slow lope after he had passed the wagon. He grinned a little, wryly, as his second thought took form. Maybe she wants to advertise, and promptly forgot her.

Ed could not account for the guilty feeling that would not let him alone. Hell, the old man had as much as invited both Phil and himself to keep their noses out of the ranch business. Why, then, should he feel guilty because he had done just that?

There had never been any lack of good feeling between Ben and his two sons. A slight natural resentment, perhaps, because the two boys were forced to believe that their father lacked confidence in their capabilities. Still, he treated them right; they had the run of Gunsight Grant, plenty of money to spend, could work or idle as they chose.

In Ed's case perhaps the resentment was greater than in Phil's. Ed loved the big ranch; he liked working with cattle. But he had stopped working on the ranch because he'd felt, with justification, that he should be more than just another 'puncher working under a foreman. Now, for some reason, he was realizing that his stand had been based on pride alone, that the time was coming when old Ben would be gone, when the running of the huge ranch would fall on his shoulders and Phil's.

At the corral, he put up his horse, then tramped to the darkened house. At the foot of the verandah he halted abruptly. From the garish gloom that illuminated the yard, he caught a movement, a sound.

Staring, he waited. A horse had come down off the knoll behind the house, a riderless horse. He was not wandering uncertainly toward the corral. The saddle on his back was plain and his color. . . .

Ed Malloy broke into a run. Halfway across the yard, certainty brought a long yell from his throat, a yell that penetrated the bunkhouse walls and brought from there a protesting murmur.

"Maier! Come here!"

He caught the horse, old Ben's dappled gray. The reins were broken, frayed.

Maier, in long, red flannel underwear, stepped to the bunkhouse stoop, and stopped to pull on his pants and boots. He grunted loudly enough to be heard across the yard: "Damn you, Ed, you drunk again?"

Ed said: "Where's Ben, Joseph? This is his horse, but where's Ben?"

III

A lamp was lighted in the bunkhouse. Joseph Maier, the Gunsight foreman, crossed the yard and stared stupidly at the gray for a moment. He put out his hand and felt the mount's hide. Then automatically he led the animal into the corral and began to unsaddle.

Ed sprinted for the house. He burst inside, going at once to old Ben's ground-floor bedroom. The bed was smooth, untouched. Ed rattled the office door, and could hear the creak of bedsprings from within.

He shouted, alarmed now—"Hirons!"—and tried the door. It was locked.

Frowning, he shouted again. A key turned in the lock, and Lenny Hirons stood there in a white nightshirt. Lenny's face was alarmed. It was also terrified, but Ed did not distinguish between the two emotions. He asked: "Have you seen Ben to-night? His horse just came in, and Ben's bed ain't been slept in."

Hirons rubbed his eyes, which did not look sleepy. He yawned.

Ed grabbed him by the shoulders and shook him. "Damn it, I asked you a question! Where's Ben?"

Hirons yanked himself free. His eyes showed fleeting anger. He said: "How the hell should I know? He goes as he pleases and don't ask me. I ain't his keeper."

Ed turned away. He heard a creak on the stairway, saw

Sarah Montano in nightgown and robe, looking down at him. "What is it?"

Ed said: "I don't know yet, Sarah. But Ben's gone." Her face was white, her eyes wide. The shapeless wrapper could not conceal the full-rounded promise of her body. Her lips, slack with sleep and surprise, were beautiful. She came on down the stairs, but Ed was gone. He slammed the door viciously behind him.

In various stages of undress, the crew was trooping toward the corral. Joseph Maier had sent one man out to bring in the horses. Ed caught his own horse and slammed the saddle up. He cinched it down.

Maier muttered: "We'll play hell finding him before morning. Can't backtrack his horse in this light."

Ed asked: "Something bothering Ben tonight? It looked to me like that gray came from the direction of Old Baldy."

Maier shrugged. "Not that I know of. He acted all right at supper."

From the horse pasture came the thunder of hoofs, and one of the 'punchers ran to open the corral gate. Thirty horses pounded into it, milling, biting, and kicking. The 'puncher slammed the gate and shot the bar into place.

Now the other 'punchers, by this time fully dressed, moved into the corral to rope mounts. Ten minutes later, Ed and Joseph Maier rode up onto the knoll behind the house at the head of a score of men.

In the first gray light of dawn, Ed looked down at the crumpled body of Ben Malloy. At first glance he had thought that Ben had been thrown. Reflection told him almost instantly that this conclusion was absurd. The gray's bucking days were over. There wasn't a gentler or more reliable horse on Gunsight. Ed got down then, saw the blood seeping through Ben's light coat. He knelt, touched Ben's cold face, then peered at a bullet hole in Ben's coat. Black powder grains were imbedded in the cloth around the hole. It was scorched from the heat of the blast.

Ed looked up at Maier. Shock had whitened his face. His eyes seemed sunken into their sockets. His mouth was grim. He said: "There'll be another hole in him somewhere. Whoever did it knocked him off his horse with the first shot. Then walked up to him, shoving the rifle against him, and let him have it a second time." He dismounted and knelt by old Ben on the other side. He touched the powder grains on the old man's coat. Then he unbuttoned the coat and laid it back. Ed could see a second stain now, low on old Ben's abdomen.

Ben's face was frozen in an expression of surprise and shock. His body was stiff. Ed felt a burning sensation in his eyes, and knuckled them until it went away. He was cursing steadily in a low, monotonous voice. He stood up. "Send a couple of the boys back for a wagon, and a man for the sheriff."

"You'll play hell getting it up here, Ed. Better pack him out on a horse."

"No. Get a wagon. I won't lay him over a saddle like a damned rustler. Get a wagon." He looked around at the boulder-strewn park. "Keep your men from milling around. I don't want the tracks messed up."

Walking carefully, he began to circle the old man's body. The clouds in the east began to take on a pale, salmon-pink color. He caught a gleam of brass on the ground, and stooped. A brass cartridge case. He picked it up, grunted— "Thirty-Thirty."—and put it down again.

Now he could see, in the growing light, the faint scuff of a boot in the hard ground. He sighted a line between the cartridge case and the boot scuff and walked that way. A few moments later, he was looking down at the ground where the ambusher had stood. Here the ground was well scuffed, as though the killer had waited for some time. But there was no single decipherable print. He thought: *I'll leave it for Miguel. He's better at this than I am.*

Careful to erase no tracks, he went back to where Ben lay. He said: "Whoever it was knew he'd be here, so he must have seen him ride away from the house. Can you account for everybody last night, Joseph?"

A frown furrowed Maier's bushy brow. He stared at the crew, mentally checking off each man. Then he asked: "Who ain't here?"

A man said: "Crockett ain't, nor Heck."

Another muttered: "Slim ain't."

Ed said: "Crockett's in town. I saw him there last night."

Maier said: "Slim's out at the Icewater Creek line camp. Heck's with him."

Ed asked: "You hear anything last night?"

Maier shook his head. "Luke was playing and singing. I didn't even hear Ben go."

Ed shrugged resignedly. Then he sat down to wait for the sheriff. He was blaming himself. Old Ben had an enemy who hated him enough to kill, and Ed had not known he had an enemy in the world. It showed him suddenly how little he had been a part of Ben, of Gunsight. He thought: *If I'd only been able to do the things he wanted more like he wanted them done.* He realized at once that such a thought was unfair. It was Ben who had done the pushing away, not he, not Phil. It was Ben who had been impatient, independent. He wondered if Ben had regretted that before he died, and he wondered suddenly if he would ever know who had killed Ben. There seemed so little to start with. A suspicion that someone had known him well enough to guess accurately where he had gone, but nothing else. Nothing else at all.

He sent Maier and most of the crew back to the ranch. When the wagon came toiling up through the timber, preceded by the ring of axes as two men cleared the way for it, Ed went down to help. They drove the wagon right to old Ben's body and loaded it in, covered it with blankets. Only then did Ed feel free to go.

He met Miguel Fernándo less than a mile from the crest of Old Baldy, and accompanied him back to the scene of the crime. They found where the killer had tied his horse. But the ground was dry and hard. There was no trail to follow. Even if they had been able to find the trail, Ed suspected the knowledge would have netted him no more than he had already guessed. The trail would have led straight back to Gunsight.

The crew and the foreman were accounted for. That left Swigert, the cook, Sarah Montano, and Lenny Hirons, the bookkeeper. Ed discarded Lenny Hirons at once as a possible suspect. Lenny hadn't the guts to kill a beetle. He discarded Swigert as quickly. Swigert was sour, irascible, sharp-tongued, and nagging, but he had been with the old man since before he had bought Gunsight Grant. He was loyal if no one else was loyal.

Sara Montano. She was all that was left. Ostensibly she had been old Ben's housekeeper, but Ed knew, and the country suspected, that she had been more than that. An outlet for the old man's physical need—nothing more. Perhaps Sarah had wanted to be more, perhaps she had wanted to share in Gunsight when the old man died. Perhaps he had refused. Or perhaps he had not refused, and Sarah had been too anxious.

Ed knew that time and patient questioning alone could unravel the mystery. It angered him to think that daily, until the murderer was discovered, he might be talking to him, perhaps even eating with him. He thought suddenly: *Phil's got to know about this. And I want to talk to John Forsberg.*

Miguel gave Ed a sympathetic smile, saying: "I want to talk to Hirons . . . and to Sarah Montano."

"All right. You go ahead to Gunsight. I'm going to town."

As Ed rode past the canvas-topped wagon at the edge of town, a girl climbed out of it. Apparently Ed and his horse intruded in a corner of her vision, for she turned her head to stare at him. Ed touched the brim of his hat. Curiosity stirred in him. Miners, and sometimes miners' families, were common enough around Fernándo. A lone girl was not, especially one as beautiful as this. Ed twitched the reins and rode over to her.

At once her eyes showed him a wary expression. Her lips tightened slightly.

Ed removed his hat. He grinned down at her. "Hello." This one did not look the sort he had hastily judged her to be last night. Still, a man could never tell. He said: "I saw your wash hanging out last night. Woman's clothes and boy's clothes. No men's."

His grin began to fade before her hostile regard that said plainly: *Let me alone. Go away.*

He said: "Fernándo is a tough town. Don't advertise the fact that you're alone."

He thought some of the grimness left her face. She said: "Thank you for your concern." There was faint irony in her voice. "I can take care of myself."

Ed shrugged. "Maybe. No offense. I just wanted to be helpful."

Some of the tautness went out of her body. "All right." She gave him the ghost of a smile.

She was beautiful in a thin-faced sort of way. Her cheeks were hollow below high, finely shaped cheek bones. Her eyes were too old for her years, too disillusioned, too wise. Ed's glance dropped, roved her body, which was slim, even slender, but rounded in the right places. When he looked at her face again, it had hardened. Her eyes were old and wise again, saying: *You're like all the rest. Go away.*

He felt a touch of irritation. He put his hat back on and swung away. He was thinking: *Good God! What does she expect? She's a beautiful woman in a country that sees damned few of them.* He made himself put her out of his mind. At the edge of town, however, a twelve-year-old boy, shuffling barefooted in the dust, made him remember her again. He waved briefly at the boy, thin-faced and sallow, and rode into town. The boy toed the dust and stared after him.

IV

Ed Malloy racked his horse before the Drover's Hotel, a huge affair, three-storied, with a long verandah that made an L, extending across the front and around one side. It was painted a pale yellow. Ed went into the lobby and glanced through the wide arch into the dining room.

The smell of coffee was pleasant in the air. Phil Malloy sat at a table by the window, a stack of wheatcakes before him. Phil was shorter and with a lighter complexion than Ed. Already, at twenty-three, he was beginning to get plump. Ed walked over to him, pulled out a chair, and sat down. The sight of food made him enormously hungry.

He said: "Hello, Phil. My God, I'm hungry!"

Phil gave him a close glance. "You look like hell. You been up all night?"

Ed nodded, and his face turned grave. He stared at Phil for a moment. Finally he said: "I've got bad news for you. Ben is dead. Somebody killed him with a Thirty-Thirty last night on top of Old Baldy."

He did not miss Phil's instant start of surprise, nor did he miss the hooded look of caution that came immediately afterward. Then came Phil's disbelief.

He said: "That's not a good joke, Ed, so early in the morning."

"It's no joke. Ben's dead."

Phil stared at him for a long moment. Then he asked, his

voice dim and low: "Who killed him?"

"I don't know. Somebody who knew his three trails. Somebody who has the run of the ranch. Somebody who could have seen him leave and circled around ahead of him and laid an ambush." His voice mirrored a growing, helpless anger. "Gut-shot him with the first shot and knocked him off his horse. Wasn't satisfied with that. Walked over and put the rifle against his chest and shot him again."

Phil shoved his plate away, took out a cigar, and bit off its end. Ed noticed that his brother's hand shook noticeably as he held a match to the cigar and frowned.

The waitress came over to the table, a middle-aged, graying woman. Ed looked up. Phil said: "Bring me some more coffee, will you, Edith?"

Ed added: "I'll have the same breakfast Phil had, Edith."

Ed was beginning to realize with something of a shock that he knew as little of his brother Phil as he had known of Ben. They were a family grown apart by the divergence of their interests. In boyhood, Ed and Phil had been close enough, but with maturity they had ceased to interest each other. Phil seemed interested more in matters of trade and business than in ranching, while talk of business and money was a bore to Ed. So, he realized, each had sought out his own kind, with the result that they saw little of each other and understood less. He could see as well that something was bothering Phil. Something that had appeared only after his revelation of Ben's death. The inevitable suspicion that crossed his mind was at once shocking to him.

Ed had a sudden emptiness inside. Grief had been strong in him this morning when he had found Ben's body, and he was beginning to understand with a shock that he was utterly alone now. He was beginning to regret that he had not been closer to his father, that he had not remained closer to Phil.

Phil stood up, scowling: "Where is he, Ed?"

"Ben? They're bringing him into Gunsight in a wagon. Why?"

"Why, I want to see him." His eyes evaded a meeting with Ed's. He turned and went to the door. A few moments later, Ed saw him striding across the street toward the stable, hurrying.

Edith brought a tray and began to unload dishes in front of Ed. She murmured: "He ordered more coffee, and he forgot to pay. Is something the matter, Mister Malloy?"

Ed said: "Somebody killed Ben last night, Edith. Phil's upset about it. I'll pay for his breakfast."

He began to eat. But the edge was gone from his hunger, and worry nagged at his mind.

Phil rode into Gunsight in mid-morning. From the direction of the blacksmith shop he could hear a saw, and the sound of a hammer pounding nails. The crew was grouped before the bunkhouse, subdued, talking in low tones. They stared at Phil surreptitiously.

He rode at once to the porch and tied his horse to the porch rail. He mounted the steps and went into the house. Old Ben's body was lying on the long horse-hair sofa covered with a blanket. Then, in the semidarkness of the room, Phil saw Sarah Montano sitting in a chair. He could hear a rustling of paper from the ranch house office, and supposed that Lenny Hirons was in there.

Phil went over to Sarah and stood looking down at her. She was pale. Her glance was gentle, a little sad. He caught himself wondering if Sarah could hold and fire a rifle.

He said: "Ed told me."

His glance was wondering, speculating. Sarah flushed. She got to her feet, a woman in her late twenties. There was a well-rounded maturity to her body.

She said: "You are not thinking . . . ?"

He stared at her, and anger began to grow in her eyes. Phil said hastily: "I didn't say that."

"But you were thinking it. Weren't you?"

He turned sulky. "Maybe I was. But who could it have been? Lenny?" He laughed harshly.

Sarah looked at him helplessly. "Do I have to defend myself to you?" He failed to answer, so she murmured in a dull voice: "I went to bed about nine. I woke up when Ed came home. I didn't hate Ben, Phil. I loved him. I couldn't kill him. Oh, Phil!"

Tears welled up in her eyes. But she held herself stiffly, waiting for Phil to make the first move.

Phil had hated Ben. He admitted it now. He had hated Ben for the way he owned Sarah, for the way he used her. He had hated himself for falling in love with her. He had known the torture of believing that Sarah was Ben's woman—infrequently, perhaps, but still too often. He had known shame because he had loved her, because he had wanted her himself. He had feared Ben's biting scorn that would have been heaped upon him had Ben found out. Phil could imagine what Ben's words would have been. *Her? Why you damned stupid pup. A man don't fall in love with a. . . .* Phil would have hit him before he'd have let him say that word, applying it to Sarah. He would have hit his own father.

Now Sarah turned away from him. There was an unaccustomed sag in her fine shoulders. The moment was past, and Phil found himself regretting that it was. He should have shown her his faith in her. He should have taken her in his arms. But he had not. All he had shown her had been suspicion. He knew suddenly that Sarah had not killed Ben. He knew he was a fool for even suspecting her.

Her back was toward him. He walked across the room and put his hands on her shoulders. "Sarah."

Listlessly she replied: "What?"

"We can't talk here. Meet me this afternoon at the lake." There was humbleness in his voice, and pleading for forgiveness.

Sarah Montano seemed to stiffen. For a long while she was silent. Finally she shrugged helplessly, said—"All right."—and walked across the room to the stairs.

In town, Ed Malloy mounted the outside staircase to John Forsberg's office. It was an untidy clutter of law books, papers, cigar butts, and ashes. A musty odor of stale tobacco smoke lingered in the air. Forsberg sat at a roll-top desk and, as Ed came in, swiveled his chair to face him. He was a small man, rotund of body, but sharp of face and features. There was shrewdness in his cold blue eyes.

He said, his voice dry and precise: "Hello, Ed. What brings you to see me?" He put emphasis on *me*. Ed felt again, as he had so many times before, a stir of dislike for the lawyer. He said: "Ben's dead, Mister Forsberg. He was murdered last night."

Forsberg half rose from his chair, and it creaked under his weight as he sat back down. His eyes widened, and for an instant his mouth was slack. Then it firmed like the jaws of a steel trap. Ed could not doubt that his surprise was genuine.

Forsberg asked: "Why, for God's sake? Why?"

Ed shrugged impotently. "That's what I don't know. I thought you might have some ideas. Outside of Ben and Lenny Hirons, I guess you know more about Gunsight's business than anyone else."

Now Forsberg did stand up. He went to the window and stared down into the street. His voice was filled with quiet amazement. "I can't believe it. I just can't. Ben was like . . . he was like something that goes on forever. I never thought of him dying."

Ed felt a lessening of his dislike. He said: "Ben was impatient with Phil and me. He ran Gunsight by himself, so neither of us knows much about how things were. Before we can find his killer, we've got to have a reason why someone would want to kill him. You think about that, Mister Forsberg. You may come up with something."

Ed told him how he had found Ben's body, how he figured it must have been someone who had known Ben and Ben's habits well.

Forsberg asked: "What about Sarah?"

"She was in bed when I came home about two this morning. She sure looked like she'd been asleep. I don't reckon a woman could sleep much if she'd just killed a man."

"How about Hirons?"

Ed laughed contemptuously. "You can quit thinking about him. He hasn't got the guts to wring a chicken's neck."

"The crew?"

Ed frowned. "They're all accounted for but Slim and Heck. They were supposed to be out at the Icewater Creek line camp. Miguel's probably checking on them right now."

Forsberg hesitated. He spoke reluctantly. "Phil?"

Ed scowled. His anger leaped like a flame. "Damn you!"

Forsberg's stare halted him. The lawyer said: "Maybe you didn't know it, but Phil wanted Sarah. He's been seeing her."

"How did you know?" Things began to fall together in Ed's mind, but he didn't want to believe them.

"I've seen them together. Sarah rides a lot, you know. She meets Phil at the lake over on Brady's Flat." His eyes took on a hot, vicarious pleasure. "I saw them swimming there not over a month ago . . . naked." He laughed.

Ed saw beaded sweat on the man's upper lip. He could scarcely control his disgust. He turned and tramped down the stairs without replying. But deep in his stomach was a sick feeling of dread.

V

Standing at the bottom of the stairs, Ed Malloy hesitated. He looked at his horse, racked before the hotel. He looked downstreet, saw the garish sign of the **Criterion**. Above the word **Criterion** was painted a nearly naked woman, supposedly representative of the pleasures to be afforded nightly inside. Ed grinned mirthlessly. The picture was hopeful. None of the Criterion's girls could match its full-blown bustiness.

Suddenly he felt the need for a drink. His talk with Forsberg had left a bad taste in his mouth, as had the revelation that his brother was cavorting with his father's kept woman. Decisively he strode along the walk and banged into the saloon. At this time of day it was nearly empty. Sol Rhodes, fat and oily, was restocking the free lunch counter. A single customer stood at the bar, a glass of beer before him.

Sol left the lunch counter and waddled over behind the bar. "Hello, Ed. Early for a drink, ain't it?"

Ed nodded. He felt a certain reluctance to relate the story of Ben's death to the bartender. Sol set a bottle and glass before him, and Ed quickly poured one and downed it, poured another.

Ed didn't know where to start in looking for Ben's murderer, unless he started with Phil and Sarah Montano, and he didn't want to do that. So far, Phil was the only one with a motive for killing Ben—Phil, or possibly Sarah. Ed doubted if Sarah could have slept last night if she had killed Ben. He also doubted if she could have feigned that look of surprised sleepiness, that look of having just been awakened. Which left Phil under suspicion.

Sol had not returned to the free lunch counter, but stood looking at Ed. Ed asked: "Where the hell was Phil last night? Did you see him at all?"

Sol replied: "Yeah. Early. He left here about nine, I guess."

Ed was suddenly ashamed of himself. He knew that if he had questions to ask, he should ask them of Phil himself. He downed his second drink and poured his third. He visualized Phil, firing at Ben from ambush, then walking over, and poking the rifle muzzle into Ben's chest and firing again. He shook his head, frowning.

Behind him the batwings swung open, admitting a large square of bright sunlight. For a moment Ed did not turn, but when no one came up to the bar, he turned curiously. The girl from the wagon at the edge of town stood there before the doors. She looked uncertainly from Ed to Sol, and on to the lone drinker at the far end of the bar.

Sol asked: "You looking for someone, miss?"

She shook her head, pale and wordless, patently scared half to death. Hesitantly she advanced across the dirty floor. Her voice was tight and thin as she said: "I'd like to speak to the proprietor, please."

Sol, unfriendly, said: "That's me. What's your beef, miss?"

"I want a job."

Sol's deep laugh rolled around the room. The girl was looking about with a kind of horrified fascination, at the cracked bar mirror with the bullet hole in its center, at the back room, at the piano that was barely discernible there. Ed felt sorry for her.

Sol broke off his laughing. "Uhn-uh. You ain't the type, sis. You go on over to the hotel and get a job slinging hash."

"I tried there. I tried everywhere else, too."

Ed could tell she was close to tears. He was beginning to feel embarrassed.

Sol waddled out from behind the bar. His apron front was greasy and black. He had not shaved for two days, and a stubble overlaid his oily skin. When he grinned, he showed a gap in his front teeth, memento of a recent brawl.

Ed had watched Sol hire girls before, so he knew what was coming. Sol said: "Come over here and let me look at you."

The girl advanced timidly, her eyes wide with fright. Ed knew he ought to interfere, but then the thought occurred in his mind: *If she gets scared bad enough, maybe she'll stay away from saloons and dance halls*. He watched, his face beginning to show anger in spite of himself.

The girl reached Sol. Sol looked down at her and said: "What's your name?"

"Sally."

"Sally what?"

"Never mind. Sally is enough."

Sol said pedantically: "In here a girl's got to know how to take care of herself. She's got to know how to push the customers away without making them mad. I doubt if you can do that."

He was panting slightly with his anticipation. His hot little eyes roved over the girl, stripping her and gloating over her nakedness. A look of revulsion crossed Sally's face, to be instantly replaced by a scared smile. Her pointed breasts rose and fell with her frightened, quickened breathing.

Ed pushed himself away from the bar. Sol's arm shot out with incredible speed, imprisoning the girl. His right arm locked behind her shoulders, drawing her close against him.

His left slid down her back, low, so that her body was forced tightly close against his obese bulk. His head dropped, and his lips caressed the girl's bare neck. Then, as suddenly as he had seized her, he released her and stepped back.

He chortled huskily: "I like my girls to be friendly with me. Reckon you can do that?"

Ed, halfway to the pair, stopped abruptly, flushing. He had been close to making a fool of himself.

A long shudder ran through the girl's body. But when she lifted her glance, there was a forced smile on her lips. She said: "Not that friendly. If I wanted that, I wouldn't have to come here looking for it."

Sol began to chuckle. He turned his back on the girl, waddled back behind the bar. He said: "You'll do. You'll do. Come to work at eight."

The girl said: "Thank you." She gave Ed a brief glance, apparently read aright his expression of outrage. Her smile faded, and she turned toward the door.

Sunlight outlined her briefly, and then she was gone. Ed tossed off his drink and rang a dollar on the bar. Then he went out himself.

She was walking, almost running, toward the edge of town. She was a nice girl, a pretty girl. She was bitter and disillusioned, but that was all. Ed wanted to do something for her, but he knew he'd be misunderstood. Misunderstood? Or understood?

He asked himself some searching questions. Why are you interested in her? Why don't you want to see her go to work in the Criterion? Because you want to sleep with her yourself?

He let his mind dwell on that for a moment, and finally shook his head. No. He was interested in her as any man is interested in a pretty woman. But he did not immediately want her. She was too hostile, too cold. He knew what the progression would be for her if she took Sol's job. Downhill, gradually, until she was hard as nails, until she was no longer a dance-hall girl, but a bagnio girl. She was bitter now. She would be more so in a month from now.

He turned back to the hotel. When he got there, he untied his horse and swung up into the saddle. He could see the straight shape of the girl, nearly to the edge of town now. He rode that way, holding his horse to a trot. He had no particular plan in mind. But he felt he ought to try and dissuade her from taking the job she had just paid for so dearly.

He came up beside her and reined down to a walk. He asked: "Have you tried Satterfield's store? Chang's restaurant?"

She nodded, her eyes hooded and unfriendly.

Ed said: "I'm Ed Malloy."

She was silent, her eyes on the ground. She kept walking.

Ed had a sudden idea, felt foolish, but knew he would advance his offer anyway. Even if she ridiculed him for it. He said: "My father was killed last night. He had a housekeeper out at the ranch, but I have an idea she'll be leaving. If you're really wanting a job, you can have that one."

She stopped and looked up, her eyes cold. She said: "And you like your housekeepers to be friendly with you. Is that it?"

Anger blazed in Ed's eyes. "No, that isn't it! You damned little. . . ." He stopped, the word unsaid. There was no desire in his eyes, no male interest as he looked at her, only plain, unconcealed dislike. He said: "Try drinking water sometime instead of vinegar." He roweled his horse's ribs, and the animal sprang away.

He was fifty feet from her when he heard her cry: "Wait!"

He went another fifty feet before he turned. Then he reined the horse in and came around. He rode back to where she stood.

Hostility was gone from her eyes. So was all her suspicion and doubt. He noticed that her eyes were gray. He saw that they could be soft as well as hard. Her full lower lip was trembling. She said—"I'm sorry."—and tried to smile. "Is that job still open?"

Anger went out of Ed. "Sure."

"How do I get there?"

He pointed up the road. "Follow that. Turn off when you see the buildings on your left."

She said: "All right." She hesitated, and finally she smiled. It was the first real smile he had seen on her face. It took all the hardness out of her; it made her truly beautiful. She said: "Thank you, Mister Malloy."

"Sure." He dismounted, and fell into step beside her, leading his horse. "I'll help you hitch up your wagon."

An awkward silence fell as they walked. But her nearness was pleasant. Ed began to think about Phil and Sarah Montano. His face darkened. He thought about old Ben. He could not account for the feeling he had that Ben's death was not an isolated incident, the feeling that Ben's death would set in motion a whole chain of events, none of them pleasant. Nor could he rid himself of a suddenly growing feeling of unease, of foreboding.

VI

Three miles to the north of the house, a ridge crossed the Gunsight Grant, perhaps a moraine left by some ancient glacier. Not a high ridge, it bisected the grassy valley. On its far side, the land seemed flatter, and less than a half mile beyond the moraine was a lake. Years before, a family named Brady had squatted beside the lake and built a cabin. The cabin was still there, a low, log affair with a sod roof. No trees grew beside the lake, only low brush, waist-high on a man.

Phil Malloy topped the ridge in the afternoon, and stared across the flat at the cabin below. A herd of deer browsed through the brush a hundred yards from the cabin, and by this Phil knew that Sarah had not yet arrived.

He rode down off the ridge, into the knee-deep grass that covered the flat. He dismounted before the cabin, and tied his horse under its pole beam overhang, out of sight from the ridge behind the cabin. There was no longer any need for carefulness, but carefulness was a habit grown in him during these last months.

He began to think of Sarah. He began to think that secrecy was no longer a need in their meetings. He thought: *I'll move from the hotel back to Gunsight. We can get married.*

The revelation of their relationship at this time would provide not only the sheriff with a motive for Ben's murder, but also the valley people with food for vicious gossip. He reflected with a slightly flushing face that whatever they said would be true. Sarah had been Ben's woman whenever Ben wanted her. She had also been Phil's on those days when she met him at the lake. He had begged her to quit Ben, but she had refused. He had threatened to give her up himself, but his threat had left her refusal unchanged, and in the end it had been Phil who had backed down.

His horse raised its head and nickered, and Phil sprang to his feet, excitement setting his blood to pounding. He stepped out from behind the cabin to see her riding downslope off the ridge. She sat her side-saddle lightly and came on at a trot. Phil was smiling as he reached up a hand to assist her to the ground. For an instant she was close to him, and with one hand still holding the reins of her horse he put his arms around her and pulled her close.

He could feel her breath, warm and sweet, in his face. He could smell her elusive fragrance. He said huskily: "Sarah, I never really thought it was you. I. . . ."

His lips met her soft ones, and his heart began to pound. Full-bodied and strong, she arched against him until his brain was afire. She seemed to draw the will out of him the way she had drawn the resistance when he had tried to make her give up Ben.

Phil drew away. He led her horse over to the cabin and tied it there. When he turned, she was walking slowly toward the lake. She stopped at its edge. A light breeze blew across it, warm and sweet-smelling from the grass it had touched on its way here. Sarah raised her face into it, raised her arms and stretched.

Phil could not understand her. He could not fathom the thoughts that stirred behind her soft, unreadable eyes. Between them, it seemed, was but one thing, the irresistible lodestar of sex.

It was enough. Breathing faster, Phil walked swiftly

toward her. He came up behind, and his arm circled her waist. He dropped his face and nuzzled her throat. His hands caressed her firm, hard-tipped breasts. He said hoarsely: "Let's go for a swim."

She nodded. At first, months ago, Phil had worried about this. This was a lonely spot, not often frequented by Gunsight's riders, except at roundup time. Yet he had felt there was always a chance that someone would ride this way and discover them. He had never mentioned his fear to Sarah, for he was wise enough and old enough to know that fear of discovery will turn any woman cold. He took off his shirt and threw it on the carpet of grass. He sat down and pulled off his spurred boots and socks. Sarah, her back to him, was also undressing. When she was through, she threw him a teasing glance and splashed out into the lake.

Phil cast a glance at the ridge, then followed her. For a hundred feet the lake bottom sloped gently away. His eyes clung hotly to the glistening perfection of Sarah's body—long, smoothly rounded buttocks, slim waist, finely formed shoulders. She turned and laughed at him, her breasts quivering with her splashing, awkward movement through the hip-deep water. Then she dived forward and began to swim.

Phil caught her near the center of the lake. He caught her ankle, and she jackknifed in the water and flung her arms about his neck. Together they sank through the clear water, her lips hot and searching. The touch of her body against him, after the cold water, was scalding. Only the need for air brought them apart. Phil's head broke the surface, and his lungs drank air thirstily. With her hair streaming about her face, Sarah came up beside him, breathed hastily, and set out swiftly for the shore. Phil followed, panting raggedly.

He splashed out of the lake, running, ten feet behind her. She was laughing now, and Phil was laughing, too. There was a spot far from the lakeshore where the brush made a small hidden pocket, where the grass was deep and soft. She sank down here, laughing and spent, and Phil sank down beside her. Their lovemaking was a glorious, endless miracle. The sun and their exertions dried their bodies. Afterward, Phil got up lazily and went after their clothes.

When he returned, the goodness was gone from his mood, and he was scowling. Withholding her clothes, he stood looking down at her. His glance ran the length of her body, admiring, faintly bitter.

He asked: "Was it like that with Ben?"

She came to her feet, concern and pity in her eyes. "Oh, you poor darling! You poor fool! Did you think . . . ?"

"That you were Ben's woman?" he supplied coolly. "Weren't you?"

She brushed her damp hair away from her face with a helpless gesture. Then her eyes widened with complete comprehension, and her mouth began to tremble. She dropped her glance, and, when she again looked up, her expression was humble. "You loved me, thinking that?"

Phil nodded sulkily. Sarah took her clothes from him and began to put them on. As she dressed, she said: "I was many things to Ben. I kept his house and took care of his clothes. I read to him, and I talked to him. I gave him companionship and respect, but I never gave him what I give to you. When you wanted me to quit him, I thought you wanted me to leave his house. I had no idea. . . ."

When you live with an idea, when it tortures you awake and asleep, it dies slowly, not suddenly. Perhaps doubt showed in Phil's face.

Sarah said: "You don't believe me."

He shook his head. "I don't believe you, but I want to marry you."

Momentary sympathy, fleeting gratefulness showed in Sarah's soft eyes. But she shook her head. She said: "There's no real love without faith, too."

Phil took a step toward her, but she backed away, shaking her head.

"No, Phil. I want to go. I'm not sure I want to see you again."

He tried to protest, but she turned and ran. With his boots in his hand, Phil ran after her. But the brush cut his feet cruelly, and he had to stop and pull on his boots. By the time he reached the cabin, she was halfway to the ridge, riding as though the devil rode at her heels.

VII

John Forsberg, after Ed Malloy had left, sat slumped in his swivel chair, feet up on the desk. Occasionally he scowled. But mostly, his expression was one of recollection, of reminiscence.

He was thinking of Ben, of Gunsight Grant, of the Fernándo family. He was thinking of the way their lives and fortunes were intertwined. He could remember long ago when Ben Malloy had been a small but moderately prosperous rancher, operating on the fringes of the Gunsight Grant. Ben could not have operated there without the good will of the Fernándos. But he had their good will, and Forsberg was remembering how he had acquired it.

María Fernándo, then sixteen, was a lively girl, an active, outdoor girl. She made living a misery for her *duenna,* escaping the rigorous supervision at every offered opportunity. One particular day, nearly fifteen years ago, she had ridden off from Gunsight alone.

Gold had been discovered shortly before in the lower reaches of Icewater Creek. There were not many prospectors who had worked their way up into the park to the Grant, but there were a few. And María was young and beautiful. One of the miners, a big, raw-boned man, bearded and red-eyed from too much whisky, slipped up on her at noon while she was dismounted and eating her lunch.

Ben Malloy, riding, had heard her screams. He pounded into the little clearing where María was fighting the prospector. He dismounted and yanked them apart. He proceeded to batter the prospector's face until the man was nearly blind. The prospector yanked his gun, and Ben killed him.

After that, María had been content to stay with her *duenna,* and, after that, Ben Malloy had been like a son to old Rodriguez Fernándo. It explained why Malloy had been able to buy the Gunsight Grant, why he had been able to pay what he had down on the place, why the Fernándos had been willing to take a huge mortgage for the balance.

Over the years, the mortgage had been substantially reduced, but it still represented a sizable fortune. Forsberg smiled. A sizable fortune that now belonged to him. Forsberg was the only lawyer in the town of Fernándo. He enjoyed the trust of the Fernándos, and got their business. It paid him well. Also, he had enjoyed Ben Malloy's trust, and had got Ben's legal business. Miserly and penurious, John Forsberg, with no family to provide for had, in the ten years he'd been in Fernándo, amassed a considerable stake. Through handling the Fernándos' legal affairs, he had naturally known of the mortgage on the Gunsight Grant, and, when he had enough money, he had approached the Fernándos and bought the mortgage as an investment, a fact of which Ben Malloy had not been aware.

Forsberg began a slow, impatient rapping on the arm of his chair. His fingers drummed ceaselessly, and his brain seethed. There was opportunity in Ben Malloy's death for Forsberg, but, so far, a way to utilize it evaded him. Impatiently he stood up. He put on his hat and coat. He slipped a short-barreled Colt revolver in the side pocket of his coat and went down the stairs.

He judged it had been an hour since he had talked to Ed Malloy. He got his horse at the livery barn, mounted, and rode out. He wanted to talk to Miguel Fernándo, the sheriff. He wanted to talk to Lenny Hirons. He wanted to talk to Sarah Montano.

Opportunity was near for John Forsberg, but he needed to add to his store of knowledge before he could seize it. He had to know who had killed Ben Malloy and why.

He rode out of town in the early afternoon and took the road toward the Gunsight Grant ranch. Three miles along the road, he overtook a rickety wagon, canvas-topped, with a twelve-year-old boy at the reins. The boy was sallow and thin, appearing vaguely familiar to John Forsberg. The girl who sat beside the boy was something else altogether. Perhaps twenty-six, she was beautiful.

John Forsberg stared at her. She was too thin. Her eyes were too wise, too old for her years. Forsberg's lips felt dry, and he moistened them with the tip of his tongue. The girl looked away from him, her face cold and still. Forsberg could feel himself flushing. He rode on past.

In mid-afternoon, he came to the ranch. Someone had built a pine casket, and it sat in the shade on the long verandah. Forsberg raised a hand at the knot of 'punchers in the yard as he mounted the steps. No one waved back.

He knocked on the door and, when no one answered, walked on in. He saw old Ben's body, blanket-covered, on the horsehair sofa. The room was semidark, the heavy drapes at the window drawn. Forsberg heard a sound from the ranch office and went toward it.

Lenny Hirons sat at his littered desk. He had a ledger open before him and was staring at it vacantly. Sweat beaded his forehead and upper lip. When he heard Forsberg's step, he looked up, startled. He was pale. He nodded at Forsberg curtly.

Forsberg pulled a chair toward the desk and sat down,

facing Lenny. His tone was unctuous, grave. "A terrible thing. Who could have done it?"

Lenny looked at him, wildness in his eyes. "I don't know. There doesn't seem to be a reason." He tried to meet Forsberg's eyes, failed, and looked away.

"How long have you been here, Lenny?"

"A year." Lenny's nervousness seemed to increase. His voice rose as he asked: "Why all the questions? Hunt up Miguel Fernándo and ask him what you want to know. I just keep Gunsight's books."

"Will you be staying now?"

Forsberg could sense Lenny's unusual jumpiness, and it puzzled him. His opinion of Lenny coincided with Ed's and Phil's opinion of the man. Lenny was gutless, a coward. He was sallow and unpleasant. There was nothing in Lenny that anyone could like. Forsberg wondered why Ben had tolerated him. *Probably felt sorry for him,* he decided.

Lenny shrugged. "I don't know. That'll depend on Ed and Phil, I suppose. If they want me to stay, I'll stay."

Forsberg got up. He said: "Ben kept his affairs pretty much to himself. Neither Ed nor Phil knows much about what makes Gunsight tick. They'll probably want to go over the books. They'll probably want me to help them."

Lenny started visibly. His hand began to shake. He laid down his pencil and gripped the edge of the desk. Forsberg's eyes widened with surprise and his sudden suspicion.

He began to smile, and asked, his tone faintly needling: "Any reason why I shouldn't go over the books with them, Lenny?"

Lenny jumped to his feet. His expression was panicked. His voice was shrill. "No! Why should there be any reason? Anybody can look at my books, mister . . . anybody!"

Forsberg hid a smile behind his hand. Triumph glowed in

his cold eyes. He said soothingly: "All right, Lenny. All right. No call to get excited. No call to get proddy."

Lenny opened his mouth to protest. Seeming to realize that he was making a fool of himself, he closed it with a snap. He grumbled: "Just don't come around here making insinuations, that's all."

Forsberg was beginning to enjoy himself. He found a sort of sadistic pleasure in watching Lenny squirm. He was sure of Lenny now. He was sure that Lenny's books would not bear close scrutiny. He feigned amazement. "Lenny, I didn't insinuate anything. What did you think I was insinuating?"

Lenny put his hands, palms down, on the desk. His whole body was shaking. A kind of terror was born in his eyes, but there was shame in them, too—knowledge of cowardice, cowardice of spirit as well as of body, and shame because of it. Lenny knew he had given himself away. He knew that he had betrayed himself needlessly because of his own guilty conscience. The realization that there is no end to deceit and treachery was plainly in his eyes. Although Forsberg could not know it, Lenny was realizing that murder begets more murder, that thievery begets only more thievery. There was defeat in Lenny's face as he sank back in his chair, defeat and increasing hopelessness. "No," he said, "you didn't, did you? I guess I'm upset. I guess anybody would be upset, wouldn't they?"

Forsberg said: "You'll be worse upset if you don't handle yourself better when Miguel questions you than you have with me. You and I can make a deal. Fernándo won't make any deals. If you break down in front of Miguel, you'll go to prison."

This time, there was no denial in Lenny. He said: "What kind of a deal are you talking about?"

Forsberg laughed softly. "I don't know how much you've

gotten away with. But whatever it is, it's peanuts compared to what you and I together can take."

Forsberg had another suspicion, one that was slowly growing in his mind. He almost opened his mouth to mention it, but changed his mind abruptly. Even a rat like Lenny could be pushed too far. Forsberg was suddenly sure that Lenny Hirons had murdered old Ben. It all began to fall together in his mind. Lenny had been stealing from Gunsight. Ben had discovered it. It explained why Ben had ridden the troubled trail last night. It explained why Lenny had known where to find him, where to lay his ambush. A cold finger of fear traveled down Forsberg's spine. He would not dare push Lenny too hard, for if Lenny, the coward, could kill once, he could kill again.

He turned to the door. His voice was now reassuring, calm. He said: "With me on your side, Lenny, they can't touch you. Remember that when the sheriff comes. I'll be the one they come to when they want your books checked. And I'll never give you away if you go along with me." An instinct of self-preservation made him add: "But remember, Lenny, if anything should happen to me, they'd probably bring in somebody from Denver to check your books. That would be too bad, wouldn't it?"

He smiled and closed the door behind him. He glanced at old Ben's body as he went toward the wide front door. Sunlight and fresh air seemed cleaner against his face than they ever had before.

He saw Sarah Montano, graceful and light in her saddle, ride into the yard from the north. He smiled greedily and let his eyes rove over her trim figure. He knew where she had been. He knew with *whom* she'd been.

He had thought to question Sarah, but there was now no longer any need for it. He untied his horse, mounted, and set out in the direction of town.

A plan was slowly taking shape in John Forsberg's brain. He was remembering that he held the mortgage on the Gunsight Grant. He was beginning to see vaguely a way to take over the whole thing. He surrendered himself to dreams of grandeur. He imagined himself master of the Gunsight Grant. He thought of Sarah Montano. He thought of the girl on the canvas-topped wagon. They had no use for him now. But put him in the saddle at Gunsight—ah, then it would be a different story.

John Forsberg had led a lonely, largely celibate life. But that did not mean he had no desires. It meant only that his mind was given to eroticisms that would have been strictly abnormal in a man used to regular, normal outlets for his passions. His smile was fixed and almost foolish as he rode into town, his brain seething with these erotic dreams. His smile may have been foolish, but John Forsberg was not. He was exceedingly dangerous.

VIII

Malloy had fully intended to accompany Sally to the ranch, to see her properly installed there. But as they pulled away from her campsite, they met Miguel Fernándo, jogging along toward town. Ed hauled up on his reins. He turned to the girl.

"Would you mind going on without me? I'll try and catch you before you reach the ranch. If I don't, ask for Joseph Maier and tell him I sent you out."

The girl's face showed quick uncertainty. But at last she nodded. The boy, whose name was Felix, slapped the reins, and the wagon moved ahead. Some way, the sullen, sallow boy reminded Ed of Lenny Hirons.

He held his horse still in the road until Miguel rode up. Miguel flashed him a smile. "*¡Amigo!* Have you learned anything?"

Ed shook his head. "How about you?"

"Nothing. Slim and Heck were at the Icewater Creek line camp. We have no suspects, my friend, except for Sarah, Lenny, Swigert, and Phil."

"Phil's no suspect."

"Ah, but he is. Phil has been, shall we say, friendly with Sarah? And Sarah was supposedly your father's friend." He raised a protesting hand at Ed's glowering expression and said deprecatingly: "I am sorry, *amigo*. But I am the sheriff. It is my job to see that the killer does not escape. If I do not consider all the suspects and their motives, I am not much of a sheriff. Is that not so?"

Ed nodded reluctantly.

Miguel went on: "I happened to run into Phil between Brady's Flat and the ranch house. I talked with him."

"Where was he last night?"

Miguel smiled. "In bed, he says. But no one saw him go upstairs at the hotel. It was while the clerk was off for a few minutes. He could have ridden out to Old Baldy, killed Ben, come back, and slipped into the hotel early this morning. There was no clerk on duty between two and six."

Ed said: "But he didn't. Phil couldn't kill Ben."

Miguel smiled regretfully, shrugging. "Perhaps not. But Sarah Montano is a beautiful and passionate woman. If I enjoyed her favors, I am afraid I might kill for her."

"Rubbish! Ben was Phil's father. It makes a difference." He did not like the conversation's trend, so he changed it. "What about the others?"

"You are Sarah's alibi. You say she quite obviously had been asleep when you came home last night. I will agree with you in that I do not believe she could kill Ben and then come home and go to sleep. So, if you have made no mistake, I would say that Sarah is innocent."

"That leaves Lenny and Swigert."

"Swigert is an unpleasant old man. He was rude to me. But I do not think he would kill Ben. He was a stricken man, if I have ever seen one. He has been known for his unquestioning loyalty to Ben."

"That leaves us with Lenny. You reckon Lenny drank a bottle of some substitute for guts and went out and did it?"

Miguel shrugged. "It is a hard case. But be patient, my friend. I will turn up something. The law is slow and sometimes stupid. But the law does not give up."

Ed nodded more curtly at Miguel than was his custom,

and reined his horse away. He lifted the animal to a wild gallop, as though the speed could erase the worry and doubt from his mind. It was unquestionable that Phil was Miguel's likeliest suspect. Phil could prove no alibi, and he had a motive. His motive was, in fact, the strongest of all compulsions. Jealousy. Wild and reckless love for a woman who belonged to another.

He caught the girl's wagon just as it was entering the yard at Gunsight Grant. He directed her to pull up before the house. He bellowed at a 'puncher squatting in the slanting rays before the bunkhouse, then alighted from his horse and assisted her to the ground. She was looking around, eyes wide and bewildered.

Ed indicated the huge, two-storied house. "It was built over fifty years ago," he said. "There used to be a stockade around it for protection against the Utes, but that's gone now. Dad used it for corrals, and the bunkhouse is built from the stockade logs."

He knew he had an awkward moment coming when the need arose to explain Sally's presence to Sarah. He did not hurry it, for he was content to stand and watch the enraptured expression on this disillusioned girl's face.

Ed himself liked the last hours of the day better than any other time. The dying rays of the sun stained the whole world with gold-orange. The rim of mountains far to the east was a penciled line of flaming color above the waving expanse of grass. Then, in a moment's time, the sun sank behind the knoll that sheltered the buildings and threw them into violet shadow.

Sally turned with a little smile. A lamp glowed in the interior of the house. Ed was stricken suddenly with the realization that the house would be empty without Ben, that last night Gunsight had lost its heart and guiding force.

The 'puncher climbed to the wagon seat and drove the vehicle toward the corral.

Ed asked the girl: "Perhaps I shouldn't ask your name. You seemed not to want to give it to Sol."

She laughed nervously. "No. It's all right. My name is Sally Hirons."

Ed started. "That's odd. The bookkeeper here is named Hirons. It's not too common a name. Any relation, do you suppose?"

She smiled. "I doubt it."

Ed looked at the little boy, Felix, standing sullen and still in the fading light. He recalled the moment when he had felt a familiarity about the boy. The boy resembled Lenny Hirons in a vague sort of way. Ed said: "I'm not so sure. But we'll see. We'll see."

As they mounted the verandah steps, Joseph Maier drove away from the corral with a buckboard. In the back of the rig was a new pine casket. Ben's body, on its last ride to town. Awkwardly, pushed by a compulsion he did not understand, Ed removed his hat.

He turned back toward the door, briskly and abruptly. "Come on in. I'll call Sarah and have her assign rooms to you. Space is one thing we have plenty of."

The huge front room was dark. Ed struck a match and held it to a lamp wick. From the open door of the ranch office he could hear Lenny, could hear the interminable rustling of ledger sheets.

He called: "Lenny!"

Lenny came to the door, frowning.

Ed said: "Lenny, this young lady will help Sarah with the housekeeping. Her name is the same as yours, Hirons. Sally Hirons, and the boy is Felix."

There was no mistaking the instant recognition that struck

Lenny at the mention of the two given names, Sally and Felix. Nor could Ed miss Sally's immediate recognition of the name, Lenny.

Sally said, in a tight, awed voice: "Why, you're my brother! I would never have known you but for the name."

Lenny came forward, peered at her in the glow from the newly lighted lamp. He said: "Ten years makes a lot of change. Felix was two when I went away, and you were twelve."

He made no move to embrace the girl. He did not even seem glad.

Sarah Montano came down the stairs, graceful and self-possessed. Ed said: "Sarah, this is Sally Hirons, and Felix. It appears that they are Lenny's brother and sister. Sally will help you with the house, and the boy can do chores."

He smiled at Sally, crammed his hat down on his head, and went outside. For some reason the revelation that Sally was related to Hirons left a bad taste in his mouth. Wondering at this, he admitted that he disliked Lenny deeply and instinctively. There was something unclean about Lenny, something that rubbed him the wrong way.

He pondered this and, mulling over what he knew of Miguel's four suspects, understood at last that both he and Miguel had dismissed Lenny too quickly and too early. Disliking him, knowing him for a cowardly nonentity, they had been too quick to assume that he could not have killed Ben. He asked himself now: *Am I suspecting Lenny because I don't like him, or because I think he might be guilty?* He stared at the house and shook his head in puzzlement. It was a question he found difficulty in answering, because he could not honestly know.

He walked to the corral, roped out his horse, and saddled. He knew he would miss his supper, but he did not seem to care. He mounted, and guided the horse up onto the knoll behind the house. Without realizing it, he was doing just what old Ben had done last night. He was riding to ease his troubled mind, and without realizing that he did so, he rode old Ben's troubled trail.

He still did not have a motive for Lenny, and he knew that Lenny would need a powerful motive for killing Ben. Innocuous and timid, what could Lenny possibly have against a man like Ben? Ben had befriended him, had picked him up in Fernándo when he was broke and hungry. Lenny owed him a debt of gratitude.

Ed wondered briefly if Lenny could be pushed by the motive of jealousy. It was hard to believe that a man like Lenny could kill for passion. Ed thought of Sarah Montano, admitting to himself that even he had felt her attraction. Why, then, could not Lenny have wanted her to the extent that he would kill for her?

A grim smile crossed Ed's face. No. The theory would not hold water. Sarah detested Lenny and made no bones about her dislike. Yet even in that dislike might be the key. Perhaps Lenny had made advances to Sarah. Had been repulsed. Perhaps his rage, instead of turning toward Sarah, had centered on Ben.

It was thin. He had to admit that. Well, then, what other motive could Lenny have? Money? Ed's frown deepened. Perhaps. . . . Abruptly he reined his horse to a halt. It was possible. It was barely possible the idea that had just come to Ed was less ridiculous than it seemed. Lenny had not the appearance of being overly honest. Suppose he had been stealing from Gunsight and Ben had caught him?

Ed knew how Ben hated a thief. He could imagine Ben's scathing indictment if he had caught one at Gunsight. And Lenny, cowardly, but with the courage of a cornered rat, might have shot him to avoid exposure! Decisively now, Ed reined his horse around and pointed him toward the town of Fernándo. He'd talk to John Forsberg about this. Forsberg could question Lenny, and perhaps take a look at the books, and could tell him quickly enough if this theory were true.

A sense of urgency possessed Ed. For the first time since he had found Ben's body, he could feel that the end of the mystery was in sight.

IX

Characteristically penurious, Forsberg had a bed in a small room behind his office where he slept and lived. Dark hung over the town as Ed Malloy tied his horse at the foot of the outside stairway and started up. His feet rang hollowly on the wooden stairs. From the street lifted the shouts of the miners, through with work for the day, beginning their assault on the check rein of sobriety. A single lamp winked from the big Fernándo house on the hill.

Forsberg's office was dark. Ed knocked loudly. After a short wait, the door to Forsberg's living quarters opened, dimly illuminating the office. Forsberg was in his shirt sleeves, his collar open. He had some difficulty recognizing Ed in the darkness. When he did, he said: "Come on in. I was getting ready to go down to supper. Have you eaten yet?"

"No."

"Then we can eat together. I understand that Ben's funeral is tomorrow afternoon."

Ed wondered who had arranged it. He felt a moment's guilt that he had not done it himself. He knew suddenly who had made the arrangements. Sarah. Yet she had shown no open grief. He wondered if she felt any.

He followed Forsberg into the stale-smelling little back room. Forsberg located a collar button and buttoned his collar. He put on a black string tie. He ran a brush over his graying hair. Then he put on his coat.

"All right. Let's go."

Ed preceded him down the stairs. Not until they were seated at a table in the hotel dining room did Forsberg question him about his errand.

Ed said: "I talked to Miguel this afternoon. It seems he has narrowed his suspects down to four."

"Who are they?"

"Phil, Sarah, Lenny, and Swigert. I won't believe that Phil could kill his own father, even over a woman. I saw Sarah myself when I arrived at Gunsight last night, and it was obvious she had been asleep. Both Miguel and I agree that, if Sarah had killed Ben, she wouldn't be able to sleep afterward."

"So that leaves Swigert and Lenny."

Ed nodded. "Swigert is out as far as I'm concerned. He's a cranky old devil, but he was loyal to Ben."

"So you think Lenny did it?"

Ed felt just a little foolish. "I didn't say that. But it occurred to me tonight that Lenny might have had a motive. Suppose Lenny had been dipping his hand into the till. Suppose Ben had caught him. You and I both know how Ben hated a thief. He'd have been pretty rough on Lenny. He might have felt sorry for it later and, being troubled, might have taken that trail of his to think things out."

"Did Lenny know about that trail?"

Ed laughed. "Hell, everybody in the country knew old Ben's three trails. It was a kind of standing joke."

Forsberg was grave, but there was an unexpressed reluctance in him. "What do you want me to do?"

"Why, I thought maybe you ought to go over Lenny's books. If he has been robbing Gunsight, you'll discover it quick enough. And if he has, we'll get Miguel to question him about the old man's death."

"Well, I guess I could do that." Forsberg would not meet Ed's eyes. He kept his hands out of sight below the table, and Ed did not see them trembling. "When do you want me to do it?"

"As soon as you can. Tomorrow, maybe. Lenny and the whole crew will be at the funeral. If you'd go out there about noon, then Lenny wouldn't know anything about it. If I'm wrong about him, I'd feel pretty bad if he finds out I suspected him."

Ed was thinking about Sally Hirons. He could imagine her rage if he unjustly accused Lenny of anything. Sally appeared to have a chip on her shoulder, especially where men were concerned.

Edith, the waitress, brought their dinners, and for a while they ate in silence. A frown furrowed Forsberg's brow, a worried frown. Finally he said: "I hate to miss Ben's funeral, but I guess he'd understand. I'm as anxious to find his killer as you are. All right, I'll do it."

Ed finished his coffee and stood up. He wondered if he would be able to reach Gunsight before Sally retired. He hoped he would. For some reason, he wanted to talk to her tonight, to be with her. He recalled the smile she had given him this afternoon. He decided she would be a damned beautiful girl if she could get over her attitude of endless distrust.

He got his horse and swung to the saddle. He set out at a steady canter along the road toward Gunsight Grant.

As soon as John Forsberg saw Ed ride past the hotel, the lawyer got to his feet. He flung a half dollar on the table and went out into the cool night air, realizing at once that his clothes were soaked with perspiration. This way, then, went a man's dreams. Because of a vague suspicion in Ed Malloy's mind, John Forsberg was to be robbed of his chance to own

Gunsight Grant. He could, of course, go over Lenny's books and find nothing irregular. But in so doing, he risked utter ruin for himself. If later it were discovered that he had deliberately covered for Lenny, then the lucrative practice he had worked so hard to build in Fernándo would be gone overnight.

Too, if he exposed Lenny now, Lenny would babble of his complicity, would reveal that Forsberg had already known about his juggling of the accounts. Lenny would reveal the proposition that Forsberg had made to him.

Forsberg was not worried that he could be successfully prosecuted for this. Lenny's word made too flimsy evidence for that. But the seed of doubt would have been planted both in the minds of the Malloys and the Fernándos as well. Forsberg would be through in Fernándo, for no one wants a lawyer who is not above reproach.

It boiled down to one thing. He had to cover himself now, tonight, or his planning would go for naught. Forsberg was a patient man, as was evidenced by his strategy to gain control of Gunsight Grant. Necessarily obtaining the ranch through the holding of the mortgage would take time. First, he and Lenny would have to loot the ranch of its operating capital, never overly large. Then, as cattle were sold to meet the mortgage payments and other expenses, the income would be reduced and the ranch would have started its downhill trail. Once that began, the end would be in sight, the day when the mortgage payments could not be met at all. When that day came, Forsberg had planned to use the money looted from Gunsight to make an offer to the Malloys for a quit-claim deed to the Grant. All of this might have taken several years. Forsberg had not minded that prospect. He was patient. He was used to waiting, to working for what he wanted.

A weight in his pocket banged against his leg as he strode

toward his office. He slipped a hand into his pocket and touched the gun. For a moment he considered making an attempt on Ed Malloy's life himself.

Nervousness and clammy cold crawled over his body at the thought. Ed Malloy was big. He was tough and young. He was considerably better with the gun that hung at his thigh than were most men. He was not a man to be taken lightly. Forsberg knew he could not kill Ed in a fight. He was equally doubtful of his chance of killing Ed in an ambush, at least without getting caught. He'd have to get someone to do it for him—someone who was unknown in Fernándo.

He halted on the board sidewalk. He hesitated for only an instant, then reversed his direction and headed for the livery stable. He got a horse and saddle from Mike Donovan, mounted, and set out down the winding road that followed Icewater Creek to the plains.

Ten miles from Fernándo was a miner's settlement named Oro City. Somewhere in Oro City there ought to be a man who would hire his gun. Somewhere in that lawless town there ought to be a gunfighter who could kill Ed Malloy and escape afterward. With the dream restored to his thoughts, John Forsberg drummed his heels against the horse's ribs. And he began to smile.

All of his life he had abided by the law. The law had been his living. But a man is gutless who will not strike a lawless blow, he thought, when the stakes are large enough. The stakes were large enough now. John Forsberg knew he would never see another chance like this one. And all that stood in the way was a man—Ed Malloy.

X

It was ten o'clock before Ed Malloy returned to Gunsight. A lamp was burning in Lenny Hirons's room, and the office was dark. Several lamps were burning in the big front room, but the second floor was dark.

The bunkhouse was still and silent. Ed turned his horse into the corral and flung his saddle astride the top pole. He stopped at the pump and dashed water onto his face. On the back porch he found a towel and dried off his face and hands. Then he went through the kitchen into the immense dining room and on into the lighted living room.

A smile touched his lips as he saw Sally Hirons. She sat on the horsehair sofa, feet curled under her. Firelight played across her face from which all the wariness had evaporated.

Across the room, half facing Sally, sat Sarah Montano. Phil stood by the window, looking out into the pale moonlight. He turned as Ed came in.

"Where've you been all day?"

Ed shrugged. "Riding. It's surprising how much time a man can waste just riding around." He looked at Sarah. "Was it you who made the arrangements for the funeral?"

She nodded, unsmiling.

Ed said: "Thank you." He looked at Phil, wondering at the vague hostility he sensed in his brother, at the strain that was so obvious in Phil.

Sarah got to her feet. "I'm going to bed. Good night, everyone."

Phil watched her climb the wide stairway. He was frowning. Ed had a feeling that Phil and Sarah had quarreled. He wondered why.

With an impatient gesture, Phil turned from the window. He said: "Me, too."

He nodded at Ed and Sally and went toward the stairs. For a few moments, the room was silent. Ed heard Phil knock on Sarah's door, heard the murmur of their voices. Then he heard Phil's tramping footsteps along the hall and the slam of a door.

Sally started to rise.

Ed said: "Wait. Don't go up yet. Please."

He sat down on the horsehair sofa beside her. He could not miss the slight tightening of her expression, the return of wariness. He thought: *You don't think much of men. They must have given you a bad time.* "Where's the boy?" he asked.

"Asleep. He's been in bed for hours."

Ed looked at the girl. She was watching the play of flames in the fireplace. Her expression had relaxed. He thought she was very beautiful. He said: "Tell me about yourself."

For a while she was silent. Finally she said: "Mother and father died from smallpox in Dodge City when I was twelve. Lenny was older than I. He left us with a family in Dodge City and went to find work. I did housework for our keep. I stayed there four years, until I was sixteen."

"Why'd you leave?" Ed was frank, curious about this girl, interested. He tried to make his question sound unlike that of an employer questioning an employee, but knew he had failed. Sally flushed, and Ed said quickly: "Never mind. It doesn't matter. I was only making conversation."

"No. I don't mind talking about it. Their name was

Hackett. The last year I was there, Mister Hackett kept arranging accidental meetings, on the back stairs, in empty bedrooms, in closets. He couldn't keep his hands off me. I tried to push him away without making him angry, but . . ."—she shrugged helplessly—"I had to leave."

Ed's face was angry. "Where did you go then?"

"I hated to leave Dodge City. You see, Lenny had promised to come back for us." Her voice assumed a hurt and vaguely resentful tone. "He didn't even write. Perhaps that will explain to you why I was not particularly overjoyed at seeing Lenny today." She went on. "Felix was six then. I worked in a restaurant for another year. But even after I had left his house, Mister Hackett wouldn't let me alone. He would wait for me in the street at night."

Remembering these things apparently had a real horror for her. Her face had paled. She stared into the fire, not looking at Ed.

"At last we caught an emigrant train heading west. I left the train in Santa Fé. A man had died along the way. His wagon was old and rickety. I guess he had no heirs, because the wagon master gave me his wagon and team." She smiled, and looked at Ed. "You saw them this afternoon. I've patched and repaired that wagon for five years. It has been my home."

Ed's mind was filling in the blanks in the girl's life. Living in a wagon, always broke, trying always to find respectable work and not doing too well. He could imagine the men who had undoubtedly slipped up to her wagon at night. He could imagine her sleeping with a gun under her pillow to drive them away.

He admired the strength that had kept the girl fighting as long as she had. He was suddenly glad he had been in the Criterion this morning. It would have been a shame to have her gallant fight end so ignominiously. He had an overpowering impulse to put his arm around her, to let her know the fighting was done. But he knew that would be fatal. He knew she would misunderstand.

Misunderstand? He smiled. He asked himself the searching question: *What do* you *want from her? What all the others have wanted, or something more?* He let himself consider what life could mean with a woman such as this to share it with. Then he smiled again. He had known her less than twenty-four hours. He could not account for the feeling he had that he'd known her much longer than that.

A curious alchemy seemed to draw them together, one to the other. Her gray eyes were soft, her smile gentle as she got up. She said softly: "I think I will like it here. I hope you will like me."

She stood, looking down at him. He got to his feet. He towered over her a full six inches. Her light fragrance drifted into his nostrils. Fright came to her eyes and went away. He caught her to him. Her face buried itself against his chest.

She said in a small, tight voice: "This is the first time."

Ed was puzzled. She was warm and soft against him. "The first time for what?"

"The first time I have wanted a man to touch me." She looked up, and Ed's arms tightened. He kissed her and was surprised at her response. Suddenly she pulled away, almost frantic. Her tone was still and without warmth. "You should have let me take that job at the Criterion. That is where I belong."

She was flushing with embarrassment and shame. Ed pushed her back down on the sofa. He sat down beside her. His voice was harsh, purposely so.

"You've got a lot of ideas, and all of them are wrong. It's normal for a woman to want a man to kiss her. It takes more than that to make a dance-hall girl out of her. Now go on up to bed. Let the past stay in the past. Not all men are like those you have been fighting all your life. And just because you wanted me to kiss you doesn't mean you belong in a dance hall."

He got up and pulled her to her feet. She smiled at him hesitantly and went toward the stairs.

Ed watched her out of sight. He was frowning as he turned. She was a bundle of twisted compulsions. Fighting off unwelcome advances had soured her, until she could not trust her own impulses. Ed called himself a fool for bringing her here, for he knew, if she stayed, her life and his would become inextricably entwined. And he was not sure he liked the prospect. He was not sure she would bring anything but unhappiness and despair. But he knew that he would not ask her to leave. What would grow up between them was one of the inevitable things.

He blew out the lamps and tramped wearily up the stairs to his room. But he did not sleep. He lay awake, turning over the day's events in his mind and searching for a solution to his many problems.

Forsberg returned to Fernándo near midnight. In his more penetrating moments, he was appalled at the forces he had set in motion. But when these thoughts came, he justified himself by dredging up what he considered the unfairness of fate in arousing Ed's suspicion of Lenny Hirons. Like Ed, he did not sleep. He kept going over in his mind his meeting with the gunman he had hired.

The man was fairly typical of his kind, Forsberg supposed, a man of medium height and build, clad in range clothes that had acquired a shine from grease and dirt. The man had not shaved for a week. He wore a long, tawny, cavalry mustache that was stained with tobacco. He smelled of stale sweat, tobacco, and spilled whisky. But there was no mistaking the stamp of him, the wildness. His mouth was thin and willful, his eyes as cold as glacier ice. His gun was clean and carefully oiled, and his gun belt and holster shone glossily from the saddle soap that had been worked into the leather.

Forsberg paid him a hundred in gold, and was to pay him another fifty, this to be mailed to a post-office box number in Denver. The man's name was Will Stiner.

Forsberg lay tossing in his bed, considering the consequences of what he had done if something went wrong, if it should be discovered that he had hired Stiner. He tried to convince himself: *Nothing will go wrong. Stiner knows his business.*

He got up, put on a ragged robe, and lighted a cigar. He sat in darkness, staring down at the lights of the town. Saloons were closing along the street. A couple of drunks, supporting each other, staggered toward the tent city at the edge of town, singing. The Fernándo house on the hill was dark.

Forsberg finished the cigar and went back to bed. For another two hours he tossed. He began to sweat, and threw off part of the covers. But at last he fell into a fitful, uneasy sleep. He dreamed. He saw Ed Malloy, gun in hand, eyes hard and cold, facing him. He saw the spurt of flame from Ed's gun and felt the tear of the bullet into his belly. He screamed.

He sat up abruptly. The town was utterly still. Out on the Gunsight Grant, a pack of coyotes yammered. In the far distance, a cow bellowed. The moon was low on the western horizon.

Forsberg got up and lighted another cigar. By the time he had smoked it down, the eastern horizon was streaked with gray. He breathed a sigh of relief. He could stay up now. He would not have to try to sleep any more.

He waited until the whole sky was gray, then lighted a

lamp. He shaved and dressed carefully. With daylight, he began to feel more hopeful. He had no reason to believe, he told himself, that Stiner would fail him.

The plan was simple. Ed expected Forsberg to go over Lenny's books in his absence. Forsberg would ask Ed to leave the funeral early, to meet him at the edge of town. But Forsberg would not be waiting. Stiner would.

Furthermore, no suspicion of Ed's murder would attach either to Lenny, who would be at the funeral, or to Forsberg, who would be at Gunsight. After Ed's murder, it would be believed that whoever had killed Ed had also killed Ben. From there on, Lenny would be in the clear entirely, and Forsberg's plan to seize Gunsight Grant could proceed as he had planned it.

XI

When Ed Malloy awoke, he could hear a bustle of activity downstairs. His bedroom door was ajar, and the smell of coffee, emanating from the kitchen, brought him out of bed. His hair was tousled, his eyes dazed from sound sleep. He heard a woman's voice, softly singing somewhere downstairs, and the sound brought a smile to his wide mouth.

He slipped on his trousers and boots, shrugged into a clean shirt. Then he went downstairs. Sally Hirons was dusting. She wore a clean, starched house dress that shrinkage had made snug. Her body was young and lithe, her breasts firm and pointed. She gave him a shy smile. Ed paused, looking at her. He stretched, and yawned. He rubbed his eyes. Then he went on out to the pump on the back stoop.

When he came back in, Swigert had his plate on the table and was pouring coffee into a mug beside it. Swigert scowled sourly. "Pretty damned soft, I'd say. Breakfast whenever you want it."

Ed started to grin at him, but then realization that Swigert was grieving for the old man made him sober. Swigert's seamed old face was as sour as ever, yet there was an unaccustomed aloneness, a deep, puzzled hurt in the old cook that was plainly evident to Ed who knew him so well.

Swigert grumbled: "Why'd anyone want to kill old Ben? Can you answer that one, son? Why'd they want to kill a man like Ben?"

Ed answered seriously: "I don't know. That's what makes it so hard to find whoever did it. I can't figure out the reason for it. Ben didn't have any enemies. We've got no settler problem." He frowned, and shrugged.

Swigert sat down across from him and sipped cold coffee from a tin cup. He asked: "What's Miguel say? Has he got any ideas?"

Ed shook his head. He heard a commotion in the yard. He drained the last of his coffee and went to the door. John Forsberg was getting down from a buggy. The lawyer approached the house.

Gunsight's cowpunchers made a sober knot before the bunkhouse door as they watched the lawyer. They were scrubbed until they shone, and each man wore his best.

Forsberg's manner was unctuous as he approached Ed. He said: "A sad day for Gunsight, Mister Malloy."

Ed frowned lightly. He hated insincerity, he hated a display of false feelings. He could sense that Forsberg felt no great grief over Ben's demise. This feeling made his voice curt. "What's on your mind, Mister Forsberg?"

Forsberg took his arm and drew him away from the house, out across the yard. He said: "Just this, Ed. I'm worried about being missed at the funeral. Why don't you come away after the church part of the service and meet me at the edge of town? Then I can tell you what I have discovered, if anything, and you can make arrangements with Miguel for questioning Lenny. Also, I can make an appearance at the cemetery for the last part of the service."

"You seem mighty sure you're going to find something."

Forsberg started, then shrugged. "Well, I'm fairly sure. I have been thinking about it." He was silent for a moment. Then he said: "It's customary to read the will immediately after the service. Will you tell Phil, and Sarah, and Swigert to come to my office when it is over?"

"All right."

Ed could feel no interest in the arrangements Ben had made for the disposition of his property. It seemed right that Swigert and Sarah should have been mentioned, Swigert for his unfailing loyalty, Sarah for the comfort she had given Ben in his declining years. But Forsberg had not finished. "Gunsight goes to you and Phil, Ed. Ben left Swigert a thousand acres and a hundred cows. Sarah gets five hundred dollars."

Before he could stop himself, Ed said: "That's not much for Sarah. After all, she was. . . ." He halted, impatient with himself for his unthinking speech.

Forsberg gave him an insinuating smile, saying: "Perhaps Ben repaid her while he was living."

Ed said curtly: "All right, Mister Forsberg. I'll tell Phil and Sarah and Swigert. And I'll meet you at the edge of town." He turned away, vaguely upset and uncomfortable, disliking Forsberg. He wondered: *What the hell did Ben see in him?*

Forsberg climbed into his buggy, and drove away. Ed had an oddly uneasy feeling, as though something unclean was in the air. He saw young Felix Hirons sitting beside the woodpile, whittling. He walked that way, wondering if the boy were like his older brother.

Felix looked up. Ed realized that what he had thought was sallowness in the boy was not that at all. It was pallor. The boy must have been ill. He was thin and sharp-faced, but his shy smile reminded Ed of Sally immediately.

Ed asked: "What you making?"

"A gun."

The boy held out his handiwork. He had a broken-handled pocketknife in his other hand, a dull knife with but one broken blade. Ed took the roughly shaped gun, looked it over. Life had been tough for Sally. He had not previously considered that it had been tough on the boy as well.

Ed handed it back. He said: "It's good. It'll be better when you get it finished." He took the boy's pocketknife, fished a small whetstone from his pocket, and honed up the knife. Then he handed it back.

He happened to think of the old percussion Derringer in Ben's dresser drawer. He said: "My dad had an old gun. It doesn't work, but how'd you like to have it for a model? Then you'd know just how to make yours?"

The boy gave him that shy grin again. "Well, I guess I would. If you don't want it no more, that is."

Ed nodded. "All right, I'll get it." He headed back toward the house.

He thought of Sally and of the boy Felix. He realized that what he wanted Forsberg to do was underhanded and, if successful, bound to hurt both Sally and the boy. He suspected it would be cause enough to send Sally away from Gunsight. But the cards had been dealt. He had to play the ones he held. If Lenny were guilty of Ben's death, not Sally, or a hundred Sallys, would save him from Ed's vengeance.

He attributed his uneasiness to the complexity of matters here at Gunsight. He could not suspect that before evening he would ride into a professionally planned, carefully executed ambush.

All the way back to Fernándo, John Forsberg wore a worried frown. Suppose Will Stiner did not show up? Suppose he simply took the hundred in gold already paid him for killing Ed, and rode out of the country? Forsberg was not particularly concerned about the money. It was chicken feed by comparison to the stakes that depended on Ed Malloy's killing.

But he was beginning to feel desperately afraid that some hitch would upset his plans.

Therefore, when he rode into town, he returned the buggy to the livery stable and headed at once for the Criterion. There, he judged, would be the most likely place to start looking for Stiner. The place was crowded with men who had known Ben Malloy, who had come to Fernándo today for his funeral. But Stiner was not in evidence. Forsberg had a drink, which was necessary to preserve appearances, then made visits to two more saloons. Fear and worry drew deep lines across his forehead. *Damn Stiner, anyway!*

He climbed the outside stairs to his office. The door was ajar. The smell of one of his own good imported cigars greeted Forsberg's nose as he stepped into the littered and dingy room.

Stiner sat in John Forsberg's own swivel chair, his booted feet up on the desk. His spurs had made deep gouges in the oak desk top. He looked up at Forsberg insolently.

Forsberg said angrily: "What are you doing here, you damned fool? Suppose someone were to see you? Suppose someone saw you come up?"

Stiner grinned. He rolled a cud of tobacco from one cheek to the other, and spat on the floor. He put the cigar back into his mouth and drew deeply. He blew the smoke in John Forsberg's face.

Forsberg's intemperate anger cooled abruptly. Something like a shiver traveled along his spine. Stiner wiped his long cavalry mustache with the back of his hand. He slid a hand under his shirt and scratched at the mat of hair on his chest. When he grinned, he exposed yellowed, stained teeth. "Nobody knows me in this town. Don't get excited."

"What do you want?"

Stiner squinted at him. "You didn't tell me how big Ed

Malloy was hereabouts. It makes a difference, my friend. You can kill an ordinary 'puncher and nobody puts up much of a squawk. A *hombre* like this Malloy is different. Besides, this proposition of yours has got a bad smell. You didn't tell me, either, that somebody plugged old Ben Malloy." His eyes narrowed until they were thin, cold slits. His mouth was cruel. "You wouldn't be figuring on making Will Stiner pay for that, would you?"

Forsberg's voice was a croak. "No! What gives you that idea? Nobody's going to pay for anything. I thought you were smart. I thought you'd be able to get away afterward. It's no skin off your nose if people think that whoever killed Ed must have killed Ben, too."

Stiner showed him an unpleasant smile. "Did you kill Ben?" he sneered. "I wouldn't have thought you had the guts."

"No!" Forsberg's protest was almost a cry. "I didn't kill Ben!"

Stiner was as cruel as a house cat playing with a crippled mouse. His grin widened, but it was not a pleasant thing to see. He murmured thoughtfully: "Something tells me there's money in this business. Big money. I can smell money whenever I look at that sly face of yours." He showed his teeth in a silent laugh. "If there's anything Will Stiner likes, it's money."

"You've been paid!" Forsberg knew with a sinking feeling that his protest was useless. Stiner had dealt himself into John Forsberg's game. Forsberg suddenly wished he had never thought of this. He'd had a solid, substantial law practice in Fernándo. He had a substantial amount in the bank. He held the mortgage on the Gunsight Grant. Perhaps this scheming would have proved unnecessary if he'd allowed events to take their normal and natural course. A bad financial panic would have brought him the Gunsight Grant, or a bad slump in the cattle market. A bad blizzard would have done the same thing. He said: "Hell, I've changed my mind, anyway. Just forget the whole thing."

"And the hundred you paid me?"

Forsberg swallowed. "Keep it. Keep it. Only get out of here and let me alone."

Stiner flicked the ash carefully from his cigar. Forsberg saw that he had stuffed his vest pocket with six or eight more of them. Then Stiner shook his head. He said firmly: "Uhn-uh. You gave me the cards in this game yourself. I guess I'll play them the way I see them."

Panic raced through Forsberg. He said excitedly: "I'll put the sheriff on you! I'll tell him you're planning to kill Ed Malloy."

Stiner laughed scornfully. "No, you won't. You won't open your mouth." He got up from the swivel chair lazily. He cuffed his hat back on his head and looked at Forsberg insolently. He said: "I'm going out and kill Ed Malloy. Then I'm coming back to see if I can't figure out some way to share the loot with you."

Forsberg slumped into his swivel chair and listened to the beat of the man's steps on the stairway. The seat was warm from the killer's body. John Forsberg began to swear and to tremble. He wished he had never seen Fernándo or the Gunsight Grant.

XII

Lenny Hirons saw Ed come downstairs. He saw him pause and smile at Sally. He did not miss the vulnerable look that Sally gave Ed who stretched and yawned like a contented cougar. Lenny ducked back into the office before Ed turned.

Ed's obviously rested condition vaguely angered him. Lenny himself had laid awake half the night, worrying about John Forsberg, about the knowledge that Forsberg held over Lenny's head. Lenny had sought frantically for a solution to his predicament, finding none. Suddenly, out of nowhere, the solution came to him. It was built upon the vulnerability of Sally's look at Ed. It was built upon the attraction of a lonely man for a beautiful woman.

Surely, if this were worked carefully, Sally could maneuver Ed into asking her to marry him. Once Sally was Mrs. Malloy, then Lenny's position at Gunsight would be secure and unassailable.

In the presence of his new worry, Lenny had stopped worrying about Ben and Ben's murder altogether, except that, whenever he thought about them, he got a vague and obscure feeling of pride. He had convinced himself that murdering Ben had proved his courage. He was not a coward at all. He was a man who could hold up his head, secure in the knowledge that he had held the power of life or death in his hand, and could hold it there again.

This, in itself, provided an out for Lenny so far as John

Forsberg was concerned. He would string along with Forsberg, so long as he needed the man to throw suspicion of Ben's killing away from him. When Forsberg got too insistent, or too domineering, then Forsberg would get what Ben Malloy had got.

Lenny smiled. He heard Ed bang out of the kitchen door, heard the clatter of dishes as Swigert cleared off the table. He could hear Sally's light, clear voice singing softly as she worked.

Lenny Hirons had never intended to return to Dodge City for her. That explained why he had never written. He'd had no intention of saddling himself with a ready-made family when it was hard enough for a single man to keep body and soul together. But now that she was here, now that it appeared she could be of help to him, he knew it would be only good sense to go out and talk to her, to repair his fences where her good will was concerned.

Feeling already a lightening of his problem, Lenny shoved aside his ledgers, got up, and went out to where Sally was working. He was diffident and shy as he sat down on the arm of the huge horsehair sofa. He thought he sensed a certain resentment in her. He said: "It's a small world, isn't it, Sis?"

She shrugged. "It seemed big enough sometimes when Felix and I were all alone. I'd have left Dodge City a long time before I did if I hadn't remembered your promise to send for us."

He tried to smile. "I wanted to, all along. But it was hard going for me. Wages were low, and it cost so darned much to live. I'm sorry, Sis. Maybe I can make part of it up to you now."

All her resentment was not gone. But it was fading. Her smile showed less strain.

He said, changing the subject swiftly: "That Ed Malloy is a

nice fellow, isn't he? Phil is, too, for that matter, but Phil's got a. . . ." He stopped, and he could feel a slow flush rising to his face. He had been about to say that Phil had a woman.

Sally was bent over a small table, dusting its top. She did not turn, but for the briefest instant her hand paused in its steady movement. She said quietly: "Yes, they're both fine men."

Lenny asked: "You going to Ben's funeral?"

She shook her head. "I hardly think it would be proper. I never knew him." She turned, frowning doubtfully. "Do you think I should?"

"Uhn-uh. You stay here. I've got to go, because Ben gave me this job."

"What kind of a man was he, Lenny?"

Lenny could not help remembering the night he had killed Ben. Recollection of the old man's contempt put a faint flush in Lenny's sallow face. He said, more shortly than he intended: "He was all right. Just like Ed will be in another thirty years, I expect." He began to feel uncomfortable under her steady regard.

She asked: "You didn't like him, did you, Lenny?"

He started to shake his head in denial. But he gave it up. He said: "No. Not much. He was the kind that'll give you a job to do, and then watch you like a hawk to see that you do it right. He was looking down my neck half the time. I didn't like it, I guess. Who would?"

He found himself squirming under her penetrating appraisal. He could not know what she was seeing—a small-minded, mean, little man with whom selfishness was a fetish. A sallow, pasty-faced weakling, whose protruding upper teeth heightened his resemblance to some bright-eyed rodent. He could not know that she was marveling that he was a brother to her and Felix, a son to the father she had admired and greatly loved. But he could see the overflow of her carefully concealed repugnance.

He thought resentfully: *My own sister!* But instead of looking to himself for the qualities that had caused her repugnance, he began to hate her as he hated all those who had disliked and belittled him in the past. He turned angrily and went back into the ranch office. He slammed the door behind him, something he rarely did. He knew at once that he had not managed himself well, but he knew, also, that however he managed himself he would not get Sally to co-operate in a deliberate attempt to trap Ed Malloy into marriage. That would have to be left to chance. Considering the obvious attraction between the two, the end he desired might well come about of itself. Yet, loose ends, to methodical-minded Lenny, were an insistent aggravation. And there were too many loose ends here.

Swigert served an early dinner in the kitchen at Gunsight at eleven. Simultaneously the bunkhouse cook banged his triangle in front of the cook shack, and the crew trooped in for their meal.

In the house sat Ed and Joseph Maier, the foreman, and Phil and Sarah Montano, Lenny and Sally Hirons, and the pale-faced boy, the wooden gun sticking out of one pocket, the Derringer visible in the other.

After dinner was over, a 'puncher brought the Gunsight surrey to the front door, and Phil handed Sarah up to the rear seat and rose to sit beside her. Sarah watched Ed climb up behind the reins, with Lenny scrambling up beside him. Swigert and Maier rode horseback with the crew.

Phil sat, stiff and cold, beside Sarah. She cast a careful side look at his stern, granite face. She longed to touch his arm, but she did not.

The surrey bounced along the road to Fernándo, and the crew fell in behind. Sarah, with moisture stealing into her eyes, thought the cavalcade made an impressive tribute to old Ben Malloy, and the phrase—"The King is dead. Long live the King!"—occurred to her troubled mind.

Now Sarah was beginning to realize that she had acted foolishly yesterday afternoon at the lake. She had continued her foolishness last night when Phil had sought to make his peace with her, and again this morning. She was coming now to the reluctant admission that Phil had gone as far as he could decently be expected to go. The next overture must come from her. Staying on at Gunsight in her capacity as housekeeper, she understood, was impossible. She had not been aware of the gossip that made of her more than a housekeeper in Ben's house. But she was aware that to continue in the position would only invite a nastier gossip that would say that she was part of Phil's legacy under the will.

Two courses, then, remained open to her. One of them demanded that she make her peace with Phil and agree to marry him. The alternative to that was leaving Gunsight forever. Pride had almost forced her already to the second course. If she persisted, leaving was inevitable. Her soft lips firmed slightly. Her eyes took on a determined look. She would swallow pride, then. Pride is a poor substitute for companionship and love. Besides that, she suspected that she was making too much of Phil's belief that she had been Ben's woman. She guessed she could hardly blame him. The whole country believed she had been Ben's. Why should she blame Phil for believing the same?

Her decision made, she moved closer to Phil deliberately. The touch of his body was hard and muscular against her. She caught at his arm and squeezed it against her. He looked at her in surprise, still holding a sulky look, but he did not draw away. She raised her face and whispered into his ear: "Phil, I'm a fool. I'm sorry."

He did not immediately smile, but when he did, all sulkiness, all resentment were gone from his face, leaving only the smile, only his complete gladness.

Sarah, never a woman to do things by halves, said bravely: "I'll marry you, Phil, if you still want me."

"Want you?" His arm went around her, pulled her against him.

They had spoken in whispers, probably unheard in the front seat by Ed and Lenny because of the noise. But with the crew riding behind them, this was not the place for a display of affection. Both seemed to realize this at once, and they drew self-consciously apart. Sarah was blushing, and Phil laughed at her happily.

He asked: "When?"

"Could we wait until Miguel finds whoever killed Ben?" She sensed an immediate cooling in him and said quickly: "It's not what you think, darling. But it doesn't seem decent for us to be so happy until Ben's murderer is brought to justice. Don't you see?"

He was thoughtful, seeming to remember suddenly their grim errand today. He nodded his agreement.

Sarah looked at Ed's straight back in front of her. She looked at Lenny's scrawny, pale neck. A small muscle twitched nervously there. Lenny's white-knuckled hands gripped each other tightly on his knees. He stared straight ahead, scowling.

At the edge of town stood a small log shack, abandoned and still. But before the shack was tied a horse, a leggy, powerful black. A wisp of smoke curled abruptly from the chimney. Sarah wondered briefly at this. Never before had she noticed signs of life about this crumbling cabin. For no understandable reason, a rash of goose-flesh crawled over her arms, and a small chill traveled down her spine. Then suddenly they were in town heading for the small white church the Fernándo family had built so many years ago.

XIII

Heads craned to look at them. Ed went into the church first. Sarah followed him, and behind her came Phil. Then the whole crew trooped in, making a racket with their squeaking boots and low coughs that was deafening in the utterly silent church.

Lenny slipped in unnoticed between two burly 'punchers. He was terrified. He was deathly pale, and shaking. But the irony of his being here gave him an obscure thrill. He had ridden in the surrey and beside old Ben's son all the way to town. He smiled faintly as he thought of this. *A man's son and his murderer riding to the funeral together.*

Up there in the front of the church was old Ben's casket. Flowers from the yards around Fernándo made a splash of color before it. Lenny sat down. He craned his neck, looking around, looking for Forsberg. He scanned each face in the church as the noise of Gunsight's entry slowly subsided. Forsberg was not yet here. Lenny began to watch the door. A few later arrivals straggled in, then at last the doors were closed and the service began.

A light frown came to Lenny's face and lingered there. A puzzled frown. Something was wrong about Forsberg's absence from the funeral. Forsberg had been the Malloy family's attorney. It was only good manners and good business for him to attend the funeral, even if he felt no particular sorrow over old Ben's passing. Why, then, was he not here?

Lenny speculated over that as the service droned on. A

woman, a town woman who had known Ben only slightly, began to cry. Lenny looked at her, and thought: *The kind that has to cry at funerals whether she knew the dead person or not.*

As his worry increased, Lenny began to fidget, and drew a hard look from the lanky Gunsight 'puncher next to him. *Forsberg. Damn the man! What is he up to?*

Lenny suddenly knew as surely as if someone had told him that Forsberg was at Gunsight. He was sitting now in Lenny's office, compiling evidence of Lenny's peculations. Lenny thought: *I'll have to kill him.*

A flush stole into his cheeks as he began to plan. Old Ben's murder had necessarily been planned on the spur of the moment. Forsberg's demise could be plotted with more care and skill. With the idea upon him, he wished to be out of the church, out in the open, where he could think clearly.

For Lenny then, the service dragged interminably, but at last it was finished. The mourners filed up past the casket, then back along a side aisle, and out the front door of the church.

Lenny was directly behind Phil who followed Sarah Montano. Sarah was weeping silently. Lenny stared at her with an inward sneer, thinking: *You're bawling for him now. But tonight you'll be in bed with his son.*

He looked around for Ed. Phil was waiting beside the driver's seat of the surrey, preparatory to driving to the cemetery. Sarah sat in the surrey, exhibiting a dignified poise. Lenny heard the quick pound of horse's hoofs, saw Ed riding downstreet away from the church, away from the direction they would take on the way to the cemetery.

Quick unease stirred the sallow little man. First, Forsberg had absented himself from the funeral. Now Ed was leaving, when custom demanded that he accompany the casket to the burial grounds. Could it be that some way, somehow, Forsberg and Ed Malloy had built some unknown evidence against Lenny?

Phil called: "Get in, Lenny." His voice was flat, exhibiting neither like nor dislike.

Lenny shook his head. He groped frantically for an excuse that would sound convincing. Panic grew in him. His mind, under such a terrific strain these past few days, suddenly refused to function at all. He threw Phil a glance that was filled with dumb terror, wheeled around, and began to walk as swiftly as he could toward the center of town, taking the direction Ed Malloy had taken.

He almost ran, at last breaking into a jerky trot. He bounded up the stairs to Forsberg's office. The office was empty, of course. Lenny ransacked the desk drawers, not knowing what he was looking for. In the bottom drawer on the right-hand side he found a gun, a Colt pocket model. He glanced at it to be sure it was loaded, then, slipping it into his side pocket, he ran down the stairs into the street.

Lenny Hirons was a deadly, dangerous man at this moment because he had no plan. His mind was functioning erratically, and all he could think was: *I've got to kill him!* He did not even know whom he meant to kill, whether John Forsberg, who had openly threatened him, or Ed Malloy, whom he felt indirectly threatened him. With the means to murder, and the will as well, he borrowed a horse from a stall at the livery barn, saddled, and took out on the road to Gunsight.

Forsberg had avoided the funeral cortège about five miles out from town by riding down into an arroyo and waiting until the procession had passed. When he deemed it safe, he came back up on the road. Dust hung in the air, the dust of the funeral cortège's passing.

Smiling, Forsberg rode on toward Gunsight. He had noted Lenny Hirons's presence in the surrey, and it had amused him hugely. For a few moments he debated whether he should go to Gunsight at all, finally deciding, however, that it would do no harm. It was desirable that he establish an alibi to cover him for the time of Ed Malloy's death. When that was done, he would worry about the menace that Will Stiner presented.

He had heard in town that Sally Hirons and her small brother were at Gunsight. She and the boy would probably be the only ones there. He would tell her that he needed to collect some legal papers out of the office. He had no intention of checking Lenny's books.

With these things settled in his mind, he went back in his thoughts to the scene this morning with Stiner. The man was dangerous. Forsberg could not deny that. But the killer was stupid, and his greed and stupidity would betray him in the end. He was useful for the moment to Forsberg, and would not be dangerous until after he had killed Ed.

Forsberg suddenly remembered that he had left his gun at his office, but he shrugged. The pistol would do him no good against Stiner. He would not risk attacking the man with a revolver. A rifle was what he wanted for Stiner, and he would not even need to conceal the killing. He could simply say that Stiner had robbed him, that he had followed Stiner and shot him as soon as the opportunity was presented. Perhaps suspicion of Ed's killing would even attach to Stiner.

He lifted his horse to a slow canter. He knew that killing Will Stiner would perhaps be the hardest thing he had ever done. The man was an animal, with the warning instincts of an animal. He seemed to know instinctively when danger threatened him. And he knew how to act when it did.

An hour dragged past, and the better part of a second hour. But at last the buildings at Gunsight took shape ahead of Forsberg.

Sally Hirons came out onto the verandah as he rode up to the house. She shaded her eyes against the glare in the yard. Forsberg was motionless in his saddle, letting his eyes move over her. *Damn these Malloys, anyway! Their money brought them the things they wanted, whether it be horses, land, cattle, or women.* Ben had brought Sarah, and now Phil had her. Ed had brought this one home. Forsberg let himself imagine briefly what this one would be like. Tardily he smiled and removed his hat. He swung to the ground.

"I'm John Forsberg, lawyer for the Malloys. There are some papers in the office I'll need before I can read the will."

The girl said: "I'm Sally Hirons."

Her expression showed him doubt and outright dislike. Her dislike angered him. Who the hell was she to look at him like that? A trollop Ed Malloy had dragged home, but wouldn't marry. Forsberg sneered inwardly. You didn't have to marry this kind.

His thoughts must have shown in his eyes, for Sally was careful to keep her distance from him as he mounted to the verandah and stepped into the huge front room.

She stayed outside, and Forsberg went directly to the office. He slammed the door behind him with unnecessary violence. He sat down at the desk and scowled at Lenny's ledgers piled high before him. He doubted if he could find evidence of Lenny's theft in the books. He was not sufficiently trained for that. But he had convinced Lenny that he could find the evidence he sought, and he had convinced Ed. That was all that was necessary.

He sat utterly still and continued to scowl. It was almost as though he were waiting for the sound of shots on the outskirts of Fernándo, the sound of shots that he would never be able to hear.

XIV

Rapidly Ed Malloy pounded over the Icewater Creek bridge at the edge of town. Ahead of him now lay only the small abandoned cabin, and then the empty miles that stretched away to Gunsight. He paused after he had crossed the bridge, half expecting John Forsberg to ride out from beneath it. He was faintly puzzled. He could not understand why Forsberg was not in evidence.

He recalled suddenly the black horse that had been tied before the old cabin, the smoke that had issued from the rusty chimney as they had passed an hour before. He shrugged, and moved in that direction. He would inquire for Forsberg at the cabin and, if that inquiry unearthed nothing, would ride on to Gunsight. It was possible, even likely, that John Forsberg had discovered something in Lenny Hirons's books that he did not want to leave, that he considered of more importance than his appearance at the funeral.

Ed felt no particular elation at the prospect of discovering that Lenny had been stealing from Gunsight. He could summon up no gladness that such a discovery would undoubtedly lead to proof that Lenny had killed Ben, but he felt anger that someone as inconsequential as Lenny could have snuffed the life from such a virile personality as Ben Malloy. He did not intend to exact personal vengeance from Lenny. He would turn the sallow little man over to Miguel Fernándo and let the law take its course, which it would surely do.

From here, he could see a tall, slim figure lounging inside the old cabin. There was nothing familiar about the figure. Ed nudged his horse with his heels, and the animal broke into a trot. When he was a couple of hundred yards from the man, Ed caught the indefinable wild stamp of the man, made out the long cavalry mustache, the faint and mocking grin.

The distance between them narrowed to a hundred yards—seventy-five. Suddenly uneasiness stirred in Ed Malloy. There was something fixed and deadly about this man's thin-lipped smile. He was fifty yards away when he halted. He could not have said why he did.

The man said: "Come on . . . come on. You're looking for John Forsberg, ain't you?"

"You've seen him?"

"Sure. He's in the cabin. Told me to watch for you."

Ed's horse was fidgeting nervously. Ed kept a tight hand on the reins. The horse swung broadside to the stranger, presenting Ed's left side to the man.

Ed asked: "What's the matter with him? Why don't he come out himself?"

This feeling of uneasiness was on the increase in him now. The stranger's stance, his cold, unwinking stare, his humorless smile—all these things carried their own warning of danger. It was nature's age-old warning system in operation, telling a man which of his fellows threatened him and which did not. Ed swung his horse, so as to present his right side to the man, so that he could dismount keeping the horse between himself and the stranger.

Will Stiner must have sensed his intent, for he yelled—"Damn you!"—and yanked out his gun. The bullet tugged at Ed's hat, and it flopped off his head as he was swinging out of the saddle, taken almost completely by surprise. But as his feet hit the ground, the heel of his palm struck the smooth-worn walnut grip of his gun. The horse was head-on to the stranger, and Ed's left hand yanked the reins, bringing around the animal's head, putting the horse's bulk between them.

Ed's gun leveled over the horse's withers and bucked against his hand. The stranger winced, and shifted his gun to his left hand with a swift, easy movement. He fired again.

Ed's horse, creased along its muscled chest, reared with a shrill snort. The reins flipped out of Ed's hand. Up on its hind legs, the horse whirled. Blood streamed down its glossy chest.

Ed stood now altogether exposed. He dropped to one knee and sighted along his gun barrel. He centered on the stranger's chest, and loosed his shot. But as he fired, the scrambling horse struck him with a flailing hoof, then was gone, pounding frantically back along the road toward town.

Ed knew the horse had spoiled his aim, might have cost him his life. The gunman's revolver coughed again, and Ed felt the bite of the slug in his side. His muscles contracted involuntarily, and he tumbled on his side.

The gunman ducked away behind the cabin. Ed started to rise, hesitated, but finally came to his feet running. His shirt, soaked with blood, clung to his side. Pain was a sharp knife digging deeper and deeper. But he made the corner of the cabin.

He ran along the wall and paused when he reached the end. He poked his head around it, quickly drew it back. The stranger was swinging up to his saddle.

Ed's drawing back had been an instinctive action that he could not have stopped had he tried. But then he leaped into the open and brought up his gun. The stranger whirled in the saddle and snapped a shot at him, and the horse shied violently. Ed fired, and then the stranger was out of sight behind the cabin. By the time Ed ran to where the man was visible again, he was out of effective range.

Ed cursed bitterly. He yanked his shirt tail out and examined his wound. While bleeding freely, it did not appear to be overly serious. He took off the shirt, made a compress out of it, tying it around his middle with the sleeves.

An odd, heady recklessness was roaring through his brain. He holstered his gun, broke into a trot, heading back toward Fernándo. His horse had run perhaps a quarter mile, then had stopped. Ed ran to within a hundred yards of it, slowed, and approached with care.

Reins trailing, the horse let him narrow the distance between them only slightly until he came to the bridge. The animal balked there, showing its instinctive fear of the hollow-sounding footing, and Ed caught it. Ed gave the horse's chest a cursory examination, deciding at once that the wound would probably not affect the horse's traveling power, and swung to the saddle.

He heard the pound of the hoofs along the road from town and, glancing that way, saw Lenny Hirons riding toward him at a break-neck gallop. But he would not waste his chance of catching the gunman on Lenny, even though he suspected Lenny of hiring the man. He yanked his horse around and touched his spurs urgently into the startled animal's ribs.

For a mile, Lenny stayed close behind him. Ed picked up the trail of the gunman's running horse without slowing down. It headed straight for Gunsight. He should have looked for John Forsberg inside the cabin before he left, he thought, but there was no time for that now.

The succession of events was puzzling to Ed. He thought the gunman could have been hired by no one but Lenny, and yet that speculation left no explanation for the gunman's knowledge of John Forsberg's name, and of his knowledge that Ed was to meet Forsberg at the edge of

Fernándo before the funeral was over.

Complicity between Forsberg and the gunman was indicated. Ed's jaw tightened dangerously. Going back in his mind over events that might have precipitated things today, he could find only one that logically could have done so—his suspicion of Lenny Hirons and his request that Forsberg examine Lenny's records. Then, if Forsberg was also implicated, it meant that he also was involved in stealing from Gunsight.

The gunman had a good fifteen-minute start on Ed. He could have got clear away. But he appeared to be heading directly for Gunsight. Ed thought of Sally Hirons and young Felix, alone at the ranch. He felt a sudden stab of fear for their safety, and urged his flagging horse to an even greater speed.

He began to see the peril of his own position. Assuming that Lenny and Forsberg were in this together, that the gunman had been hired by one of them, then upon his arrival at Gunsight Ed would face not only the gunman whose shooting was expert, but Forsberg. Both probably would be inside the stout house where they could shoot at Ed without giving him much chance to shoot back effectively. He would be delayed in the yard, giving Lenny time to come up behind him, to pour lead into his back. The only alternative was to veer off the road, ambush Lenny, then proceed under cover to Gunsight. He considered this with some approval for a few moments. One thing only decided him finally against it—Sally's presence at Gunsight.

If Forsberg were involved in Ben Malloy's cold-blooded murder, then a woman's safety would be unimportant to him. And Sally, if she received any inkling that her brother were involved in the fight against Gunsight, might feel bound by her new loyalty to do what she could to checkmate Forsberg and his hired killer.

Never in his life had Ed Malloy made the ride from Fernándo to Gunsight as quickly as he did today. Yet it seemed that the minutes dragged interminably.

He glanced over his shoulder occasionally. Lenny had apparently been unable to hold the pace that Ed set, for he kept falling back. At last he was an occasionally seen speck in the distance.

Ed could summon to his mind no plan of battle. But building within him was a cold and intolerable rage, rage that would supplant a plan. He thought of Ben, of a killer standing over him pumping an unnecessary slug into Ben's unresisting chest. And all this was over money, Gunsight's money that neither Forsberg nor Lenny was honest enough to leave untouched.

Fury would carry Ed Malloy into the fight that loomed ahead. But it would not turn the bullets that Forsberg might fire hastily, or that the stranger would aim with unerring accuracy.

XV

Forsberg heard the frantic pound of hoofs as Will Stiner approached Gunsight. Quickly snatching a .30-30 from the antlered rack above the fireplace, he ran to the door. He levered the gun to pump a cartridge into the chamber, and was surprised that an empty jacked out onto the floor. But he had no time to wonder at this. He saw Stiner coming, pushing his exhausted mount to the utmost.

The animal was covered with foam. As he reached the gate, the mount faltered, and almost fell. Forsberg raised the gun, sighted along the barrel. Will Stiner came over the sights, and Forsberg drew his bead on the man's chest.

His finger tightened down on the trigger. But he never fired. Suddenly he wondered why Stiner was in such an all-fired hurry. He stepped to the door and out onto the verandah, still holding the rifle. Stiner's horse plunged to a halt before the verandah, and the gunman slid off. The horse wandered across the yard at a fast walk, stuck his muzzle into the drinking trough, and sucked thirstily.

Forsberg said: "That horse'll kill himself drinking if you don't get him."

"To hell with him!"

Stiner's words made Forsberg realize that his concern for the horse had been purely automatic, that it was silly under the circumstances.

Forsberg asked: "What's the rush? Did you do it?"

"No. He ain't over ten minutes behind me. I knocked his hat off and got him in the side, but he's plenty able to travel."

"Then why'd you come here?" Forsberg's voice was an outraged screech.

Stiner snatched the rifle away from Forsberg, and slapped him on the side of the face with the back of his hand. "Get a-holt of yourself. You think I'd try hightailing out of the country with that jigger on my tail?"

Panic took hold of Forsberg. "What'll we do?" he wailed.

Stiner looked at him with pure disgust. "What do you think, you damned fool? We'll get him as he rides into the yard."

Stiner looked at his horse, still drinking from the trough. It was plain even to Forsberg that the animal was finished. He would be dead in another ten minutes. Stiner was looking at his rifle sticking out of the saddle boot.

He said: "Get over there and get my rifle. But don't try to use it."

Forsberg stood dumbly, not moving. His mind was overwhelmed by realization of the catastrophe that had befallen him. Stiner kicked his rump viciously. "Get moving!"

Forsberg staggered across the yard and yanked the rifle out of the boot. He came back to the verandah, and climbed the steps dazedly. Stiner's lip curled. He shoved Forsberg ahead of him into the house. He slapped the lawyer again, and put his cruel face close to Forsberg's.

"Get this through your thick skull! It's get Malloy now or go to prison. Which would you rather do?"

Forsberg murmured weakly: "Get Malloy, I guess."

Sally Hirons came down the stairs. She was deathly white, and her eyes were wide with fright. "What's the matter?" She indicated Stiner with a nod. "What's he doing here? What's going on?"

Stiner crossed the room and seized her arm. He grinned. "Who's this, Forsberg?"

"Malloy's housekeeper." Forsberg glared at her. "One of 'em. Ed's got one, and Phil's got another. You can call 'em housekeepers, if you want. I got another name for 'em."

Sally jerked her arm free. She walked over to Forsberg and slapped him. Stiner laughed. But he was not quick enough to save her. Forsberg's balled fist came out, caught her high on the cheek. Forsberg was not a big man. But he weighed a good forty pounds more than Sally did. She staggered back across the room and collapsed in a crumpled heap against a heavy oak table. Her thin cotton dress tore as she fell, exposing a long, shapely leg.

Stiner laughed again. "Not bad. Not bad at all. Maybe I'll have time for her later." He went to the front window and looked out. He said brusquely: "Get to a window in the back of the house. And you'd better shoot straight if you get the chance, my friend."

He handed the .30-30 to Forsberg. With no more talk, Forsberg slouched out into the kitchen. He punched the glass out of the kitchen window and laid the muzzle of the rifle on the sill.

It was waiting now. Waiting. Forsberg's eyes widened, and the pupils shrank. Sweat broke out on his high forehead. His knees began to tremble. Why, oh, why had he got himself into this?

His mind was dumb with terror, yet in spite of this he began to see a way out for himself. He would let Stiner get Ed Malloy, and then Forsberg would get Stiner. After that, he could talk himself out of it. Or could he? Sally Hirons must have heard his conversation with Stiner.

Sweat ran into Forsberg's eyes. He wiped it out with an impatient hand. Was there never an end to killing? He began to tremble harder, but at last he shrugged. He would have to kill Sally, too. But he could explain that easily enough. A stray bullet. . . . He heard the pound of hoofs along the hard-packed road. He peered out of the window, and his knuckles turned white against the scarred walnut stock of his gun.

Ed Malloy's horse was done. Ed ran him into the yard, to within a hundred feet of the house. Then he yanked him to an abrupt halt, and was out of the saddle in one easy motion.

Perhaps this was the moment Stiner had been waiting for. Perhaps he wanted to be sure this time, wanted a stationary target. He fired as Ed swung from the saddle. His bullet tore through Ed's saddle, broke the horse's back, and deflected on the cinch buckle on the other side.

The horse pitched to the ground, pinning Ed down by one leg. He was half exposed to the gunman in the front window, momentarily dazed from the fall. He was about to move, to wriggle himself behind the dead bulk of the horse, when he heard a shout: "Got him, by hell!"

He lay still, waiting. He lay on his left side. His right leg was free, but his left remained pinned. He inched his hand toward the grip of his gun, for this movement would be screened from the house by the body of the horse.

Let the gunman think he had killed him if he would. It was the only chance Ed had. Lenny Hirons would be coming up behind him pretty soon. And Lenny was a man who took no chances, if he were the one who had killed Ben. Lenny would stick the muzzle of his rifle against Ed's chest and make doubly sure of Ed's death.

Ed wondered what had happened to Sally. He felt a sinking in his stomach, the nausea of dread. What had they done to her? Something, certainly. She would not stand helplessly by while they poured lead at Ed, of that he was sure.

Through slitted eyelids, he saw Stiner come to the door.

The man peered at him closely. Ed wondered if Stiner could see his regular, controlled breathing at this distance. He tried to take small breaths.

Stiner came out on the porch, alert, ready. He whirled as Forsberg followed him out. Stiner said—"I'm going to be sure of him this time."—and raised the rifle.

Forsberg carried his .30-30 loosely. Suddenly he raised it slightly, holding it ready before his chest.

Stiner's rifle muzzle centered and steadied on Ed. Ed knew he was going to have to move. He knew as well that it was too late. He could not avoid Stiner's bullet. His only chance was to jerk as Stiner fired, to take the bullet in a spot that would not prove fatal. He knew a moment's panic. It was a slim chance. Too damned slim.

A high, boyishly frightened yell lifted from across the yard: "Hey!"

Stiner's finger, snug on his trigger, jerked enough to fire the rifle. The bullet tore into the ground in front of Ed. It showered him with dirt and raked a jagged furrow along his shoulder. He wanted desperately to look around at the boy, but he knew that split second would cost him his life. He lifted the heavy Colt out of the holster, yanked it around in front of him, rested the muzzle on the horse's neck.

What he saw on the porch truly amazed him. Forsberg rammed his rifle muzzle into Stiner's back and pulled the trigger. Ed's shot caught the gunman at the same instant, in the exact middle of his forehead.

The gunman's body jerked, was driven back by the impact of Ed's slug. He buckled in the middle, and his rifle clattered on the porch. Ed tried to wiggle clear. He gave his leg a desperate yank, but the boot was caught on the saddle. He pulled his foot out of the boot and got to his knees.

Dizziness held him this way for the briefest instant. When

his vision cleared, he saw Forsberg walking across the yard toward him. Forsberg held the rifle awkwardly to his shoulder. His eyes, over the gaping bore of the gun, were terrified. The muzzle shook. But Ed knew that at this range, even a man as frightened as Forsberg could not miss.

He thumbed back the hammer of the Colt. Weakness claimed him, and he could not hold the weapon. Pain throbbed from his side, where Stiner's bullet had creased it. More pain tore at his shoulder. Loss of blood blurred his vision.

Forsberg, almost running toward him now, screamed: "Die, damn you! Die! You can't walk with that much lead in you!"

Ed did not even hear the pound of Lenny's horse as it came into the yard. But he heard Felix's high yell. Ed's shoulder blades itched, expecting a slug from Lenny's gun. Ed Malloy knew he was almost done. He tried foggily to concentrate on the Colt in his hand. His eyes would not track, and instead of a single John Forsberg coming toward him, he now saw two. He thought crazily—*Which one shall I shoot at?*—and knew a sudden wild compulsion to laugh.

XVI

Time seemed to stand still. There was Forsberg, wavering rifle at his shoulder, coming on at a shambling run. Somewhere behind him was Lenny, who also would desire Ed's death. Young Felix could not stop that. Young Felix had already done more today than could reasonably be expected of a scared twelve-year-old. He had saved Ed's life by startling Stiner.

Ed shook his head, and braced himself for the impact of Forsberg's bullet. The man was only a blur now.

Suddenly he heard a scream. He remembered Sally. She was all right, then. He forced a new concentration onto his weakening mind. He raised the Colt, centered it roughly on the blurred shape of Forsberg. He pulled the trigger.

So weak was he that the slight recoil from the gun toppled him backward. He heard the roar of Forsberg's rifle, heard another rifle speak, more distinctly.

He rolled. His wounded shoulder ground into the dirt, bringing pain that was excruciating, that momentarily cleared his mind and vision. A nightmare, this, a timeless, never-ending nightmare. He wondered vaguely how long it had been since he had ridden into the yard. A minute? Five?

He turned and came again to his knees. Lenny was sliding off his horse twenty feet away. He had a short-barreled revolver in his hand. Like Forsberg, Lenny was terrified.

Ed said: "You killed Ben."

"Yes!" It was almost a scream. "He was going to send me

to prison. You hear? He was going to send me to prison!"

"Why?" Ed didn't really need to ask that. He knew Lenny had been stealing from Gunsight, and there was nothing old Ben hated worse than a thief. He knew as well that old Ben would never have sent Lenny to prison. To Ben, men were born to run free, as animals, unfettered by any restraint sterner than their own consciences.

He tried to stir up hatred for Lenny. But there was not enough to Lenny for a man to hate. There was only weakness, blubbering weakness. There was only cowardice and cravenness of spirit.

He said: "You're no brother of Sally's."

Lenny laughed hysterically. "No. She doesn't know that, though. I was adopted." He took a couple of steps toward Ed. "What are you trying to do? Nobody's going to save you, least of all yourself. You can't even raise that gun."

Ed tried. But Lenny was right. Paralysis had spread down the arm from the shoulder wound. Ed was on his knees and could not stand up. But he was damned if he'd die on his knees. He sat down. He knew he'd never make it in time, but he had to try. He brought his left hand over and took the gun from his useless right.

Lenny, fright widening from his eyes suddenly, threw up revolver and yanked the trigger. He missed. He thumbed back the hammer for another try.

Ed heard the sharp, flat report of a rifle behind him. Dust kicked out of Lenny's vest in a light puff. The little man was driven back, but his feet worked like pistons for a moment, and he stayed upright. The revolver dropped from his nerveless fingers. His eyes glazed. His expression became incredulous as he took his last look at something behind Ed.

It seemed to take forever for him to fall. But when he did, he was still. Ed sat staring at him. He heard light running steps behind him. He heard the hysterical sobbing of twelve-year-old Felix and saw the boy come running toward him.

Felix stopped before he reached Ed. His eyes were wide, his face white. He said: "Sis, don't touch him. He's dead, but he won't fall over."

Sally's voice was sharp with terror. "Felix! Stop it!" She knelt beside Ed. She cried: "Ed! Ed! Is it bad?"

He tried to smile. He looked down at himself. His shirt was gone. It was tied about the side wound, and was red and stiff with blood. Blood from his shoulder had run and spattered all across his chest. Dust had mixed with the blood, and blackened his hide.

He heard himself saying: "I've lost some blood, I guess. I don't' feel so good."

"I've got to get you to the house. I can't leave you here."

She put her arms around him, trying awkwardly to lift his weight. She got him to his knees. Felix came over, and between them they got him to his feet, started him toward the house.

The pain of movement seemed to clear Ed's head. He asked: "Forsberg?"

"He was in with that gunman. They both wanted you dead."

"Did I get Forsberg?"

"Yes. You be quiet, now."

A horse now came into the ranch yard. The rider reined up beside the trio, sheathed his rifle, and slid to the ground. He looked at the sprawling bodies in the yard. He said: "*Amigo,* did you do all this by yourself?"

Ed grinned weakly. "Not Lenny. You were just in time there. Saved my hide."

Sally protested: "Stop talking. It's not good for you."

Miguel Fernándo took Felix's place at Ed's side. They

went painfully up the steps to the verandah.

Sally said: "Take the sheriff's horse, Felix, and go after the doctor."

They laid Ed down inside on the horsehair sofa, facing the kitchen. Sally ran for hot water and towels. Miguel found a half-empty bottle of whisky. He handed it to Ed, saying: "Save a little of it for the gunshots."

Ed held the bottle to his mouth. He drank the whisky like water, in great, long gulps. Like liquid fire, it seared his throat, built a roaring bonfire in his stomach. His head began to clear. The pain of his wounds seemed lessened.

He could see Sally clearly as she returned to the room. He could see the quiet terror in her eyes as she looked at him. He could see her lips forming a silent prayer. She unfolded a clean sheet and began to tear it into strips for bandages and compresses. Then she dipped a towel into a pan of hot water and soap and came toward him.

He knew that if he had anything to say, he must say it now. He murmured: "Wait a minute." He talked almost as though he were talking to himself. "Lenny killed Ben. He told me he did. Forsberg must have been in it with him. But what the hell did Forsberg stand to gain? What was in it for Forsberg that made him willing to have me killed? That would have to be something big."

Miguel Fernándo turned from the window. He had been staring into the yard. He said: "Perhaps it has no bearing on this, *amigo*. But Forsberg owned the mortgage on Gunsight. I cannot see why he would want to lose something in which he had an interest, even a slight one."

Ed was genuinely surprised. "I thought your family owned that."

Miguel seemed apologetic. "Forsberg handled Father's legal affairs when he was dying. He told him that he needed a good investment and would like to have that." Miguel would not meet Ed's eyes. "I am ashamed for my father, *amigo*. He did not want to tell Ben, and he was too weak to refuse Forsberg's request. So he sold it to him."

It was the link needed to tie Forsberg to Lenny. Ed said: "That's it, then."

The pieces of the puzzle suddenly fell into place. A mortgage holder had no interest in looting a piece of mortgaged property unless he wanted the property instead of the mortgage on it. He said: "Forsberg found out that Lenny was stealing from Gunsight. He saw a chance to do it up right, to weaken Gunsight enough so that eventually we'd be unable to meet the mortgage payments. But when I suspected Lenny and asked him to check Lenny's books today, he knew he'd have to get rid of me. So he hired that gunslinger."

Sally's voice was firm with authority and with her worry for him. "That's enough talking from you. You're too weak."

He shook his head. "No. One thing more."

She knelt beside him. She seemed to know from the look in his eyes that he wanted to take her in his arms, that he hesitated because of the dirt and blood that was on him. She laid her head against his chest. His arms went out, circled her, and pulled her close.

When she raised her face, there was moisture in her eyes. Her lips were trembling. All of the wariness was gone from her. She was unafraid, placing herself in this man's hands.

Ed smiled. He said: "I don't really need a housekeeper. But I need a wife. Would you take the job?"

She nodded, wordless. She looked at Ed's steady smile. Then she was smiling, too. She said: "You're just trying to save money. You wouldn't have to pay me wages if you married me."

He nodded, grinned at her mockingly. "That's the only

reason I asked you. All the Malloys are smart that way."

Miguel Fernándo snorted disgustedly: "*Amigo,* that's the damnedest proposal I ever heard in my life. You. . . ."

But Sally cut him short. She said—"It was the nicest one I ever heard."—and lowered her lips to Ed's for a kiss.

Ride the Red Trail

From 1933 to 1937, Lewis B. Patten served in the U.S. Navy, primarily in the Asiatic Fleet, mostly in China and the Philippines. In December, 1938, a civilian again, he married Betsy Lancaster, and over the years had a daughter, Frances, and two sons, Clifford and Lewis B. Patten, Jr. In 1943, tired of work in a government bureaucracy, he moved his family to DeBeque in western Colorado where he spent five years as a rancher. A studio was made out of the attic in the ranch house, and it was there that Patten worked at night, writing Western stories. In 1948 he invested in a sawmill in Evergreen, Colorado and moved his family there. The Patten cattle were moved there as well, but most of them perished in the bitter winter of 1948–1949. He was determined to make writing Western fiction a career. He was quite prolific, publishing numerous magazine stories in the early 1950s, and, when he later turned to novels, he would regularly publish anywhere between three and five a year. "Ride the Red Trail" was one of his last magazine stories, appearing in *Western Ace-High Magazine* (6/54).

I

"Nance Yager"

Lew Harvey stepped onto the bare and wind-swept train platform, and surveyed the buildings of Cottonwood. His face, thin and bronzed, was tight and defensive, his dark eyes were bitter. They wanted him back, and this was a thing he could not refuse them even when he remembered the hard, harsh words that had sent him away. "You're no good, Lew," his father had said. "You're rotten to the core. Now get out! Get out of Cottonwood and get off H Spear. Don't come back! Ever!"

Now there was trouble in the Sand Hills, and trouble was Lew Harvey's business. So they unsaid all the words that had laid festering in his heart these three years past. They unsaid them and said more that came to: "We haven't changed our minds about you. But we need your rotten talents now, and you owe us your help."

A sour smile twisted his long, thin mouth that had forgotten how to make a real smile. He was a tall man, saddle-lean, with wide thick shoulders and narrow, tapering hips. He wore boots and the standard Levi's of the cow country. He wore a new sheepskin coat and a battered, wide-brimmed black hat. The sheepskin hid the guns that nestled against his thighs. But looking at the man, you knew they were there.

Behind him, the trainman called his—"Boooaard!"—and the train began to move. Lew picked up his sacked saddle and leather valise and stepped off the platform into the mud.

They wanted him back, but they wanted him to slip unseen into the back door and to do it effectively. They didn't want to acknowledge him publicly, and their hatred of him hadn't lessened.

There was perhaps a quarter mile of open ground between the town and the railroad station, and a path wound straight up the hill. Lew started up the path, but he had gone no more than fifty yards when a buckboard whirled up to the station and stopped. A girl sprang down, scanned the platform with a quick glance, and then looked up the shallow hill toward the town. She saw Lew, and at once the animation, so noticeable in her before, vanished. She was still, and cold, and motionless.

A perverse impulse in Lew said: *Make it hard for her. Make her come to you.* But there was the memory of things that had been between himself and this girl, and with the slightest of shrugs he turned around and headed back toward the station and the waiting buckboard.

Nance Yager. She was thinner than she had been, or seemed so. But she was beautiful, more beautiful even than his heart remembered. The top of her head came just to the point of Lew's shoulder. *She would be married now,* thought Lew. She would have married quickly after he had left if only to show the country that her heart was intact.

Lew approached her gravely and said: "Hello, Nance."

Her soft gray eyes were defensive, and her oval face flushed with embarrassment and the strangeness of this. "Hello, Lew."

He made a tight grin to conceal the pounding uncertainty he was feeling. "Where's the old man?"

Her clear-eyed glance fell away from his and steadied on the ground between them. Her flush deepened until it was painful. Then all at once her lovely shoulders squared, and her eyes met his defiantly. "He didn't come. He doesn't know you're here."

The impact of this was like a blow. Lew could feel anger stirring in him, and resentment, and frustrated helplessness. He stooped, his eyes blazing. "Well, I can take the next train out."

"Lew, don't. They need you."

He looked at her. "They could say so, couldn't they?"

"They're proud. And you hurt them, Lew." Her tone said: *You hurt me, too. You hurt me terribly.*

He stared at her angrily. She was clad in a wolf-skin coat that came to her hips. Her hair was copper red, throwing off glistening highlights in the morning sun. Her skin was white and smooth, her lips full and somber now. Her tongue flicked out and wet her lips.

Lew said: "You wrote the letter. I knew that. But I thought they'd asked you to write it." He stood, stilled by uncertainty for a moment, while the past came flooding back to his tortured mind. He said: "I expect you're married now. Who is the lucky man?"

"I'm not married, Lew."

"Why not? Can't you find a man that comes up to your high standards?" He knew that was unfair, but he could feel in himself a desire to hurt her—as she had hurt him.

Nance bowed her head. "I deserve that."

He knew a vast impatience. "Nance, for God's sake, what am I supposed to do? If the old man doesn't know I'm here, it means he hasn't changed his mind about me. He'll accept no help from me. What am I supposed to do, crawl to him on my hands and knees?"

She murmured: "I don't know, Lew. I just don't know. But I do know that you're the only one who can help. I didn't know where else to turn." She twisted a small scrap of handkerchief between her nervous hands. "I still depend on you, Lew. I guess it will always be that way."

She was a proud girl and had always been. Yet, today, she was humble, baring her heart to him, begging him to stay and help. Help in what? That was something he did not yet know.

He asked: "What's going on? Why does the old man need me now? He's got along for three years without me."

"He's changed, Lew. He began to change as soon as you left. He's older. The spirit's gone out of him. He won't fight, and Hans Vogel knows it. But if he has to leave H Spear, he'll die, Lew. And Vogel will have killed him just as surely as if he did it with a gun."

Vogel owned Stirrup, north of Jared Harvey's H Spear. Stirrup had started out as a small, greasy-sack outfit, but apparently now it was growing.

Nance went on. "H Spear lies between Stirrup and the Sand Hills. Vogel wants the Sand Hills. It's that simple, Lew."

"So you send for me. Suppose I take it from there. I killed a man once here in Cottonwood. I killed him in a drunken fight over a woman."

Nance winced, but Lew went on cruelly. "I liked guns, and I used to practice with them a lot. I was good, the best Cottonwood had ever seen. I killed a man with my guns, and between the town and the old man they ran me out. Didn't need my kind in the Sand Hills, they said. Didn't want killers in the country." He paused, white-faced and scowling. "Now you've got a job for a killer, I take it. You want me to go out to Stirrup and kill Vogel."

She seemed to cower like a wild, whipped thing.

Lew was ashamed, yet, somehow, he could not stop. "I kill Vogel and save H Spear for the old man. Then what do I do? Tuck my tail between my legs and slink out of town until he needs a killer again?"

Anger was stirring in Nance. She said: "It is not Vogel your father cannot fight. It's a man he's brought into the country from Wyoming. Roe Blaine."

The name drained all of the anger out of Lew. It left him empty. When you got to naming men like Hickok, Earp, Masterson, Bonney, and Short, you generally included Roe Blaine. But Blaine didn't work for nothing. If a greasy-sack outfit like Stirrup could hire him, it meant that they weren't going to fool around. They meant business, and their present business was H Spear and the Sand Hills. After that . . . well, after that the world was their acorn.

Lew shrugged wearily. "I guess you win," he said. "Let's go."

He let Nance drive and sat beside her, staring straight ahead as the buckboard left the town and took the muddy, rutted road that rose and fell endlessly on its way across the rolling, grassy Sand Hills. Occasionally he would glance at her face, so still and lovely and intent as she drove.

Once he asked—"Nance, what's your stake in this?"—and drew from her a hasty, pitying glance, and her words: "Does everybody have to have a selfish interest?"

They were quiet after that. But long before they sighted the scattered buildings of Flying Y, she said: "Perhaps I do have a stake in what happens. I have the ranch, and, if Stirrup comes into the Sand Hills, I'd surely lose it." Her words did not ring true, and Lew had the feeling that this was the first time the possibility of losing her own ranch had occurred to her.

Then they topped a certain long rise and could look down at Flying Y below. It was a tidy ranch that showed a woman's influence. In the big yard between house and outbuildings was the tip-off that this place was woman-managed, for there was an orderliness about things. Nance drew the team to a halt and nodded toward the bunkhouse. "You can stay there tonight."

Lew's mouth twisted. "And every night until my job is done. You don't think the old man would let me stay on H Spear, do you?"

She didn't reply, but started to climb down from the buckboard seat.

Lew asked: "Pepper still ramrodding your outfit?"

She nodded. "He went over to Spear today to help your father." On the ground, she looked up at his face. She begged: "Don't fight with Pepper, Lew. Please."

He shrugged. "I can't promise that. Pepper's too damned loose with his tongue. Maybe I'd better stay in town."

Her eyes darkened with contempt. "You've changed, Lew. You didn't used to run from things."

Lew knew that if he lingered, looking down at her, feeling the sudden run of his temper, that he'd do one of two things. He'd either unload all of the years' resentment on her, or he'd jump down and take her into his arms, a thing he was hungering to do in spite of all she'd done to him.

He didn't stay. He slapped the backs of the horses with the reins and drove away toward the barn. Behind him, he heard the house door slam with unnecessarily violence. The familiarity of things here struck home suddenly, and he knew pain and regret that the past was gone, that the love which had flamed so hotly in them both should have burned down to such bitter ashes.

Motion caught his eye, and he looked up to see Pepper Dixon riding in. Pepper was a middle-aged man, perhaps forty-five. He was short and wiry and as irascible as a steer in heel-fly time. He wore a perpetual, irritable frown, and his tongue was as sharp as a knife. He adored Nance Yager, and

Lew knew he'd cheerfully give his life for her.

Pepper rode into the yard, saw Lew, and reined over toward him. Recognition showed itself in his narrowing, steel blue eyes, in the thinning of his steel trap of a mouth.

He said: "You! What the hell are you doing here?"

Anger came up in Lew like a flood, as it always did around Pepper. Lew said, keeping his voice even with an effort: "I'm here because Nance sent for me. She says there's a job in the country that calls for a man, and she didn't reckon there were any left hereabouts."

He could almost grin at the way blood surged to Pepper's face. Pepper snarled: "For a gunslinger! A killer! It don't take a man to be either of those."

Lew shrugged. He was surprised that his anger was gone. All he could feel now was dry amusement. He wondered how Pepper had ever been able to make him mad and keep him that way. Pepper was ridiculous in one sense, pitiable in another. But Pepper personified the narrow-mindedness that had driven Lew from the country. Nobody had even bothered to question him, to find out what the quarrel had been about. Nobody had asked him to explain. They'd all simply drawn their own conclusions, and after a day of that the stubbornness had come up in Lew and he was damned if he'd explain anything to anybody.

Lew grinned up at Pepper, baiting him and enjoying it. He said: "Maybe you'd better move to town, Pepper. Because I'm staying for a few days until I get the job done. I wouldn't want you to feel dirtied by sharing the same bunkhouse with me."

He heard Nance's voice behind him. He turned, and she said: "I asked you not to fight with him."

"And I did anyway," he said, and faced Pepper again. "Folks need executioners, and they hire them, but they don't have to live with them or even treat them civil, is that it?"

Nance said softly: "You're feeling sorry for yourself, Lew."

"Maybe I am. Maybe I just built something up in my mind that wasn't there. When I got your letter, I couldn't help thinking that you and the old man had regretted jumping to a conclusion so damned hastily. Maybe I thought you wanted to hear what I had to say about that affair three years ago. Then I get here, and what do I find? That you sent for me because nobody in the Sand Hills had guts enough to tackle your trouble with Vogel. Or maybe because none of you wanted to dirty your hands with it."

Pepper snarled something deep in his throat and lunged at Lew. Lew side-stepped, but not before Nance's voice cut out sharply: "Pepper! Stop it!"

Pepper halted, glowering.

Nance said: "He's right, Pepper. And I ought to be ashamed." She turned to Lew. "I'll pay your train fare both ways. And apologize. I see now what a terribly cruel thing it was. And I'm truly sorry."

It was Lew's turn for embarrassment and shame. He said: "I'm sorry, too, Nance. Now let's forget it, huh?"

He had told himself for three years now that he could forget her. He had told himself that for every man there must be a hundred women he can love with equal intensity. Yet when Nance called him, he came. And coming, had dreamed the old dreams. Standing here now, he knew there could never be another for him. Never one like Nance. Watching her, he murmured silently to himself: *Funny. After all that's happened, I still want to hand her the world on a plate.*

He turned away and stepped into the bunkhouse, facing reality for the first time in three years. He had expected too much of his father and of Nance, had expected the benefit of too much doubt. He had owed it to them to offer an explanation that only his own pride had withheld. Now that he knew the mistake was his, it was too late.

With his sheepskin off, the guns at Lew's thighs stood out, plain and menacing in their smoothly oiled and cared-for precision. A grimace crossed Pepper's face as he came into the bunkhouse and saw them. He said: "Why'n hell did you have to come? Why don't you let her alone?"

"She sent for me."

"And now she's got it all to go through again. Damn you, Lew, I was hoping you'd get killed, somewhere, sometime."

"Cheer up, Pepper. Maybe Blaine will kill me."

Pepper shot him a sharp glance. He grumbled: "Maybe. It's something to hope for." He fumbled in a chest for a clean shirt, took off his soiled one, and shrugged into it. He asked sourly: "How long you going to take for this job?"

"Not long, Pepper. Maybe I'll do it tomorrow. Then you can have your bunkhouse again. You can air it out all day, and maybe by night it'll be fit to sleep in."

Pepper scowled at him, irritated by Lew's flippant attitude. Lew went out. He got a pan from the washstand at the back door of the house and went into the kitchen. From a teakettle on the stove, he half filled it with hot water, ignoring Nance who was busy with supper.

Outside, he cooled the hot water in the pan with more from the pump. Then, setting the pan on the washstand, he began to wash. He found a broken comb stuck between two of the house logs and ran it through his hair, peering at himself in a piece of broken mirror that hung over the washstand.

He saw a long, thin face, and dark eyes that held a somber, brooding look. He saw a chin more out-thrusting and aggressive even than it had been in years past. He saw the change the years had made, and suddenly liked it not at all. There was but one explanation for all the bitterness his face revealed, and he faced the explanation tonight, knowing at last that hurt and his own resentment because of the hurt had wrought the change.

Pepper came up behind him and said sarcastically: "Don't it scare you sometimes, what you see in that mirror?"

Temper flared wildly, but briefly, in Lew. With it still in his eyes, he banged into the kitchen without answering. Pepper was like a man teasing a snake with a stick, trying to make him strike. Nance must have fathomed this, for a frown of doubt creased her smooth forehead.

Lew took a chair at the table. He said: "Where's all your crew?"

"We don't have one. Vogel hired them away from us. But it doesn't matter too much. Pepper can do what feeding's needed."

"How many men has Vogel got?"

"Twelve, now. Counting Roe Blane."

"For a little outfit like Stirrup?"

"He doesn't figure it will be little any more in the spring."

"How does he plan to take H Spear? Is he trying to buy?"

She shook her head as she placed a steaming bowl of chicken and dumplings before him. Behind him, Pepper slammed the door coming in.

Nance said: "As you know, H Spear is only a hundred and sixty acre homestead claim. They hold their range by the right of prior usage. Vogel simply means to drive his herds onto H Spear grass in the spring. Then it will be up to your father to move him out. If your father can't do that, he'll be left with nothing but a hundred and sixty-acre farm instead of a ranch. And the law can't touch Vogel for it."

Lew whistled softly. "Smart."

11

"Doom Beckons"

Lew knew that Vogel would get away with it. Easily, if Lew's father refused to fight. All the range in the Sand Hills was held by right of prior usage, which meant that it was held by force or the threat of force. Each man knew that trespassing on his neighbor's grass would bring violence. They respected that. Nance had seen the single solution to the problem. Lew's father was still refusing to face it.

When he and Pepper had finished their dinner, Nance took off their plates and brought a freshly baked apple pie. She watched the two of them as they ate, her expression still and worried. "Lew, what are you going to do? Are you going to see your father?"

He nodded. He was thinking that if he failed to do this, then his father would believe he was either afraid or ashamed. Actually, he was a little of both.

He got up abruptly, picking up his hat from the floor at his side. "I'll see him tonight."

"Would it help if I went along?"

"This is something I have to do alone."

He went out into the fading day's light. He got his saddle out of the parked buckboard, dumped it out of its gunnysack, and carried it to the corral. He roped out a bald-faced sorrel gelding and threw the saddle up onto his back, and rode away in the direction of H Spear.

Riding, he tallied up all that stood between himself and

the old life, finding the gap too wide to bridge. H Spear looked as it always had looked, even in darkness. It was as though Lew Harvey had never really left it. It seemed as if he were just returning from a long day's ride, or from a trip to town.

Lew halted before the back door uncertainly. The impulse stirred in him to shed his guns now, to shed them and so ease the shock of his coming. He resisted the impulse. He had left here wearing the guns and had worn them continuously for three long years. He had come back wearing them, and they were the reason for his coming back. He would not greet his parents with a lie. He raised his hand and knocked.

He heard the movement as his mother approached the door and knew fear for the first time in his life. Real fear. Fear that made his forehead clammy, his knees weak. Fear that made his hands like ice.

The shock of seeing him could be no greater than his. She had aged ten years in the last three. Always a spare woman and small, she seemed even thinner, seemed to have shrunk in stature.

Her weathered face paled, and her nearly colorless lips trembled. She said, weakly questioning: "Lewis? Lewis, is it really you?"

"It's me, Ma. Can I come in?"

She seemed dazed, shocked. She said weakly, stepping aside: "Of course, Son. Come in. I'll call your father."

He stepped into the warm, fragrant kitchen. She backed from him, eyes wide, lips silent.

"I'll call your father." She could not seem to tear her glance from the guns at his thighs.

She turned suddenly, and fled from the room. Lew heard a murmur of voices from the direction of the ranch office. He heard his mother's rising voice, then approaching footsteps.

As Lew's father stepped into the kitchen, Lew caught a glimpse of something exalted in the wasted face. There was the flash of gladness in his father's eyes, the excitement. But that was before his eyes caught the gleam of blue steel at Lew's thighs. When he saw the guns, it was as though all life went suddenly out of his face. His eyes turned hard, the way Lew remembered they had been the day he had left. Jared Harvey said harshly: "What do you want? Why the hell did you have to come back?"

There was a soft exclamation of protest from Lew's mother. "Mister Harvey! This is your son!" Lew could never remember her calling his father by any term of endearment, or even by his given name. It was always Mr. Harvey.

Lew was shocked at the change three years had made in both his parents. Age had come quickly to them, for one thing. And the age that had come so quickly had stolen all youth and sparkle from their eyes. They were a pair of elderly people now, whose zest for life was gone. Their eyes had a dull look to them, a dull, defeated look. No wonder Hans Vogel thought taking H Spear would be easy. It would have been easy, if Lew hadn't come home.

Lew wondered at the small-boy uncertainty he was feeling. Did a man ever grow old enough and tall enough in his own right so that he didn't feel this way before his parents' disapproval? He doubted it. A smile tugged ruefully at the corners of his mouth, and then went away.

He said: "Nance Yager sent for me. She said that Hans Vogel was going to take H Spear in the spring if somebody didn't stop him. She said Vogel had brought in a gunman, and that the guts had gone out of you and you wouldn't fight. Does that answer your question?"

He had thought his father almost incapable of real anger. Now he saw that he had been mistaken. His father had not yet gone all the way down the road to defeat and senility. A spark still remained.

"I don't want your help."

Lew muttered: "You're going to get it whether you want it or not. You were always the proud one, weren't you? I think I can see now why everything happened as it did. You're the lord of the manor. Even mother is afraid to call you by your first name. When I was a kid, I can remember that there was never any way but your way. Because that was the right way. And God help whoever had the guts to argue with you." He paused for breath, the realization coming to him that he had never talked to his father like this before. He went on: "Maybe that's why I strapped on the guns. I was eighteen when I did, remember? I got tired of being treated like a damned baby. Maybe I was trying to prove something . . . that I was a man in my own right."

The whipped expression on his father's face, the expression that had replaced anger, made him feel ashamed. But he had to go on. These were things that had festered in his brain for too many years to be suppressed any longer.

"I strapped on the guns, and I practiced with them until I was the best shot and had the fastest draw of anyone in the country. You were close to the point of ordering me off H Spear when the shooting happened, weren't you? So it was easy. You never bothered to find out what really happened. You just reared back virtuously and said . . . 'I knew he'd come to a bad end.' "

Lew's mother had wrung a dish towel between her hands until it was twisted. She said fearfully: "Lewis, don't talk to your father this way."

He shot her a glance, and his eyes' hardness softened somewhat. He said: "It's time somebody did. Before I leave tonight, you're both going to know what really happened that night I killed Howie MacCambridge."

Jared Harvey said stiffly: "We know what happened."

"Sure. Sure. You know what happened, but you don't know why, or how. You jumped to a conclusion, remember? You said your son was no good, and you were secretly a little pleased that your prophecy for me had come true, that you'd been proved right again."

His mother interrupted: "If there was justification for what you did, Lewis, why didn't you tell us?"

Lew made a bitter smile. He said: "Before the smoke cleared away, several people from town ran into the livery barn. They were conclusion-jumpers, too. They saw me with a gun in my hand, and they saw Howie MacCambridge on the floor, dead. They said we'd fought over Lily Durand. The way they looked at it, it was unsavory, and their little minds liked it that way."

Mrs. Harvey said gently: "It *was* unsavory, Lew."

"Was it? Do you know what really happened? The fact is that Howie MacCambridge got Lily Durand in trouble with her family. I scarcely knew her, except to pass the time of day with her. When Howie found out she was in trouble, he came to the livery stable all set to leave the country. Maybe I was a damned fool, but, when he got to shooting off his mouth about it to me, I got mad. I figured the least he could do was to stay and see her through. I told him so. I was only a kid, and didn't have sense enough to keep my nose out of other people's business. But I liked Lily, and thought Howie was giving her a raw deal. I told him he was going to stay and stand by Lily."

The faces of the two Harveys expressed a kind of pitiful bewilderment.

Lew continued, his voice lifeless, as he remembered that black day: "Howie fancied himself a gunfighter, too, if you remember him at all. He said he was damned if a punk kid was going to mess up his life playing Galahad. He drew his gun and shot. But he missed. He was getting set to shoot again, and I plugged him.

"Well, my concern for Lily was foolish, as I found out. Howie was dead, and she saw a chance to horn in on H Spear. She claimed I was the owlhoot. And you all believed her. Even Nance believed her. Remember how noble you were about it? You were willing to forget the fact that I was a murderer if I'd put aside my guns and marry Lily. But I was damned if I would because by that time I saw how rotten Lily really was. So I went away."

Tears were spilling out of Mrs. Harvey's eyes, running across her cheeks. Her knees were trembling so badly that she had to sit down.

Lew's father looked utterly and completely beaten. He whispered: "Why didn't you tell us this three years ago?"

Lew laughed harshly. "Because you wouldn't listen. Remember the time you came to visit me in the jail? The first time you saw me after it happened? The first words you said were . . . 'I knew something like this would happen. How could you do it, Lew?' That was the attitude the whole country took. They had a juicy scandal, something to whisper about and get excited about. After the town, and the two of you, and Nance jumped to the same conclusion, I began to get a chip on my shoulder about it. I figured, if you were all so damned ready to believe me guilty, I wasn't going to disappoint you. Nobody asked me what happened. They all told me. I kept thinking that somewhere, sometime, someone would have enough faith to ask me how it really happened. No one did. Maybe I was a damned fool, but that hurt. I guess it hurt more than anything that's happened before or since. The sheriff couldn't hold me. Howie's gun was in his hand,

and it had been fired. The coroner's inquest said it was self-defense, and they turned me loose."

Lew's mother was crying. His father, still unwilling to admit so grievous a wrong, asked with stubborn defensiveness: "How do we know what you say is true?"

If anything could have hardened Lew's heart, so ready to soften and forgive, that could. He said coldly: "You don't know." He looked at them both bleakly for a moment, then turned on his heel and went out the door.

The night air was cold on his sweating body. He climbed up on his horse and reined away. He rode a full hundred yards, clear out of the yard and into the screen of willows that bordered the creek before the house door opened behind him.

He heard his mother's voice call: "Lewis. Lewis! Come back!"

But he did not turn. His face was bitter and utterly cold as he turned his horse toward Nance Yager's Flying Y.

As he rode, his anger mounted steadily. He had been a fool to come back to offer his help, help they scorned. He shoved back the skirt of his sheepskin coat and let his hands caress the cold, smooth grips of his two guns. These were his friends, his only friends. They were with him always, never questioning the things he did, but only willing to help him when he called for their help. They would earn him a living, and a good one. All right, let them earn his living. But let him never question the things they did.

He would start with Roe Blaine. To Blaine he would add Hans Vogel. And anyone else foolish enough to interfere. Then he would ride away. Blaine's name on his tally board would be impressive. And there would be others until the name of Lew Harvey was known and feared from the chill high country of Montana to the desert buttes of Arizona.

He rode, and at midnight came into the yard at Flying Y. There was a lamp burning in the kitchen. The bunkhouse was dark. Nance Yager's two dogs came rushing out at him, barking furiously until he cursed them to silence.

He turned his horse into the corral, threw saddle and blanket onto the top corral pole after an appraising glance at the sky. He tramped toward the bunkhouse, his anger burned out by its own intensity, feeling now tired and drained of feeling. But before he reached the bunkhouse, the kitchen door opened, and Nance called into the darkness.

"Lew? Is that you? Could I talk to you a minute before you go to bed?"

His lips formed his refusal. But he never uttered it. With a resigned shrug, he changed direction and headed for the house.

He came into the kitchen, and Nance was waiting nervously, her face white and taut from strain.

"How did it go, Lew?"

He asked sourly: "How did you expect it to go?"

"Well, I'd hoped. . . ." Her voice trailed off.

Lew shrugged, and his shrug expressed three years of frustration and bitterness.

"They refused your help?"

He grinned wryly. "They didn't exactly welcome it. But they'll get it anyway, Nance, don't worry about that."

She stared at him for a long moment, her eyes soft but filled with worry. "I think I'm more worried about you tonight than I am about them. H Spear is only a ranch. But you are. . . ." She seemed to be groping for the right word.

Lew's mind supplied several words for her, none of them what she sought, he guessed. *Gunslinger. Killer. Fool.*

She said: "Lew, this is a crossroads for you. I don't know what has happened to you in the last three years. I don't know what you've done, or what you've been. But I know this. You're Lew Harvey. I'm sorry I sent for you, because if you do what I've asked you to do, there will be no turning back. Roe Blaine is famous. The man who kills him will be equally famous, and a target for every gunman in the West." An expression of fear crossed her face. "I don't know how fast you are with your gun, Lew. Maybe you aren't fast enough. Maybe it's you who will be. . . ." She could not seem to say it.

Lew supplied the words. "Maybe it will be me who is killed? Maybe it will, Nance. Pepper's hoping it will."

Nance sat down suddenly, and put her hands over her face. She was shuddering, trembling. She said: "Lew, go away. I'm sorry I wrote you, and I'm sorry you came. You can't win. If you beat Roe Blaine, you'll be a marked man wherever you go. If you don't. . . ."

"I'll be a dead one," he said callously. "You should have thought of that before you wrote that letter."

"Yes." She stared up at him for what seemed an endless time. Her face seemed to lose every bit of its color. She said at last: "Lew, I knew it was wrong to write you. I knew I would be pulling you into something from which you couldn't escape. But I had to see you. Do you know what the last three years have done to me? Do you know how I've wanted you? I've told myself a thousand times that you're no good for me, but I failed to convince myself."

Lew felt a stir of excitement, and he moved a step toward her, halted himself. *Let her talk,* he thought. *Let her get all the words said.*

She murmured: "The past is gone, and we can never go back. There is probably someone else for you. . . ." She swallowed, and meeting his eyes became a visible effort for her. "Lew, I am sure of one thing now. What you did three years ago may have been wrong. I don't know. But I am sure that you did only what seemed right to you at the time. I know you, Lew. And I know you couldn't do anything you didn't believe was right."

III

"Smoking Guns"

This was the statement of faith that Lew had waited for. This was the statement that might have changed his life had it been made three years ago instead of now. But he felt a grin coming to his face, felt that and a new lightheartedness of spirit. He crossed the room in three swift strides and snatched Nance up out of her chair. Savagely he crushed her against him, savagely and hungrily lowered his lips to hers.

She responded in kind as three years of longing boiled to the surface. She was as savage as he, as desperately hungry. She pulled away at last, and the words tumbled out. "Lew, I've waited for you. There has been no one else. I knew it was useless and foolish, but I could think of no one else. Has it been like that with you?"

"Yes. Yes. But don't talk now. For God's sake, don't talk now. The past is gone, and we're starting fresh tonight."

A shadow crossed her face as she remembered Vogel and Roe Blaine. She seemed to tear the words from her heart: "It's too late! Lew, take me away with you. Tonight. Don't see Blaine, or Vogel. Don't think of H Spear or of your parents. Be selfish for once."

He asked: "And Flying Y? Will you let Vogel have that that, too?"

"Yes. Yes. I don't care about anything . . . anything but you."

He muttered hoarsely. "You said you didn't think I could

do anything unless I thought it was right, and you told the truth. I can't. Running now would be all wrong, Nance. You know it would."

Her shoulders sagged, and she stepped away. She said bitterly: "Why do people have to make such terrible mistakes . . . and go on making them?"

"Because they're people." He turned away. "I'll be back in the morning, Nance. I'm going to see Vogel and Blaine tonight."

He went out the door before she could speak. Walking across the yard, he glanced back. The lamp still gleamed from the kitchen window. He knew it would be burning when he returned—if he returned.

He was suddenly, savagely angry. He caught a fresh horse out of the corral and threw up his saddle. He cinched it down with unnecessary violence. He swung up, but, as he did, he became aware of a shadow at the corral gate. He knew a prickly feeling along his spine that vanished when Pepper's voice came out of the darkness. "Runnin' away?"

"You wish I would, don't you?"

"Uh-huh."

"Well, I'm not running. I'm going to Stirrup. And if I'm alive in the morning, I'm coming back."

"Mebbe Blaine'll get you."

"Wishful thinking, Pepper."

"Maybe I'll kill you myself, if Blaine don't. You've hurt Nance enough."

"Try it sometime, Pepper." Lew touched spurs to the horse's sides.

He had been bitterly angry upon his arrival here. He had felt the animosity in every living human he met. That animosity had stirred a bitter resentment in him. Riding, he eased his guns from their holsters, one at a time, and by feel checked the loads in their cylinders. He began to feel a growing tenseness in all his body, his brain. Unconsciously he hurried his horse until the animal was running steadily.

Lew knew this country like he knew the palm of his hand. He knew each gully, each ravine. He knew the landmarks, and so laid his course in a direct, straight line. After one o'clock, he ran past the buildings at H Spear a quarter mile away, and saw a gleam of light in the kitchen window. His mother and father were still up. And they were probably sorry, now that it was too late.

How would it go? Was Roe Blaine the fabulous gunman he was reputed to be? Or was he only a treacherous punk that had built a reputation on unfair advantage? He tried to remember all he had heard of Blaine. And found the memory elusive, vagrant.

So he concentrated on Vogel. Vogel was a short man with a nose too large for his face. Vogel had protruding, yellowed teeth and chewed tobacco. Vogel was a greedy, little man, but that made him no less dangerous. He was untidy and unclean, but if he wasn't stopped, he'd own most of the Sand Hills before he was through.

Right now, Vogel was waging a war of nerves. He'd started by hiring the crews away from H Spear and Flying Y. He'd done some talking in the saloons in Cottonwood, and had served notice this way that spring would find him moving in on H Spear. Now he was letting Lew's father worry. Giving him time to break under that worry. But Lew's father needed no more time. He had already broken.

So engrossed was Lew in his own thoughts that he did not hear the horse that pounded along in his wake until his father's yell came.

"Lew! That you? Hold on a minute. I want to talk to you."

Lew drew rein reluctantly, and waited until his father

caught up. He could not see the expression his father's face wore, in darkness.

Jared Harvey said conversationally: "Headed for Stirrup?"

"Yes."

"Mind if I tag along?"

Something tightened in Lew's throat. He said: "No, come along." This was as close as his father would ever come to apology, Lew knew. When he'd first gone away, he had dreamed at times of the way he'd make his father crawl someday. Now he no longer wanted that.

He moved out, and Jared Harvey followed. Another change, this. Always before, as long as Lew could remember, his father had led.

"Got a gun?" he asked cryptically.

"Rifle. This is your show. I'll try to keep it between Blaine and you."

In silence then they covered the miles that lay between H Spear and Vogel's Stirrup. They rode in and found the place dark.

An advantage, in a way. A disadvantage in another. Vogel and Blaine would be taken by surprise. But that very fact might prove dangerous. Men taken by surprise are more inclined to ill-considered and hasty action.

Stirrup had a house now, an addition since Lew had left. It was a small, two-room log affair, separated from the bunkhouse by a hundred feet of bare yard. Lew drew rein. Vogel surely would be in the house. But how about Blaine? Would he be sleeping in the house by virtue of his standing, or would he be in the bunkhouse with the crew?

Lew guessed he would be in the house with Vogel, and hoped his guess was correct for if it were not, the results could be disastrous. He said softly to his father: "Stay outside and keep your rifle on the bunkhouse door. Hold the crew in there. But don't take any chances if Blaine should happen to be in the bunkhouse. Understand?"

He dismounted, tied his horse to a cottonwood sapling, and advanced across the yard afoot. House and bunkhouse faced the same direction, so that Lew could see the bunkhouse door out of the corner of his eye as he knocked on the door of the house. He knocked thunderously, and heard a sleepy, protesting voice inside.

Footsteps shuffled toward the door. A voice grumbled: "What the hell you want at this time of night?"

The door opened. Vogel, clad in a soiled white, knee-length nightshirt, stood there yawning audibly.

Vogel repeated irritably: "What you want?"

"Blaine here?"

"Yeah. Come on in while I light the lamp."

It was obvious to Lew that Vogel had neither expected nor recognized him. Lew stepped into the house. Vogel's tone had changed at his mention of Roe Blaine's name.

Vogel shuffled across the room, fumbling for a match at the stove. He struck it, and in its brief flare Lew's eyes saw and remembered each piece of furniture in the room.

Vogel gasped as recognition of Lew came to him. "Harvey! Lew Harvey!"

Lew edged around so that he stood opposite the wall that held the bedroom door. He said softly: "I hear you've been talking, Mister Vogel. I hear you've been bragging that you'll take H Spear in the spring."

Vogel glanced uneasily at the bedroom door. He deliberately raised his voice. "You're damned right I'll take H Spear, Harvey! You think you can stop me?"

Vogel was scared, and it was obvious that his defiance was possible only because of Blaine's presence in the other room. Lew heard the softest kind of stir in there, and knew Blaine was awake and up. Vogel's gun and belt hung over the back of one of the kitchen chairs. Vogel began to sidle imperceptibly toward it.

Lew said: "Hold it, Hans. Hold it right there!"

Vogel stopped. His glance went to the bedroom door with a kind of frightened expectancy. Lew was silent, waiting, watching.

He kept his glance on Vogel's face, for the man stood but a half dozen feet from his gun. Lew watched Vogel, and Vogel watched the door. For what seemed an eternity they stood just this way. The tension mounted steadily. Occasionally Lew would hear a sibilant sound from the dark bedroom. He heard the faint click of a belt buckle, and smiled wryly. Blaine couldn't fight without his pants. It was part of his ego. Lew heard the scuff of a boot, and guessed that Blaine had to have his boots on, too. That was probably superstitious. Lastly he heard the slap of holster and thigh, and knew that in another moment Blaine would come through the door.

But he kept watching Vogel's sly face, waiting for the gleam of triumph that would tell him Blaine was coming. Suddenly, with sinking heart, he saw this as it would look to the country, to the law. Vogel had done some talking, but he'd made no overt move toward H Spear. Lew himself was a known killer, tried and convicted in the minds of the Sand Hills people. He was here, in Vogel's house, a trouble-seeking intruder. If he killed Blaine, or Vogel, or both of them, he would be arrested and tried for murder. And he'd be convicted, too, he realized that. He'd be hanged or sent to the territorial prison to serve out his remaining years behind bars. Nance and the normal life he'd been dreaming about would be forever beyond his reach.

Suddenly he was sickened, desperate. Yet now that he was here, what could he do but go through with it? Blaine would force him to kill, or be killed. Vogel stood ready to dive for his guns the instant Blaine stepped into the room to create a diversion. Lew had faced death before, but never this cold, ruthless certainty. In a moment Blaine would step into this room, gun fisted and ready. And the instant he did, Vogel would dive for his gun that hung six feet from his hand, holstered, over the back of a chair.

The expression Lew had been waiting for came like a flash to Vogel's pinched face. His eyes shone briefly, and his muscles tensed. In that split second, Lew thought bitterly, quietly: *You think you're good, do you? Well, you're going to get a chance to prove it. You're going to have to cripple both of them before their bullets kill you.*

He crouched almost imperceptibly, but still did not draw his gun. He risked a quick, wary glance at Hans Vogel.

Long seconds ticked away, and with their passing Lew felt the intolerable tension on the increase within himself. He tried to calm himself with thoughts of Nance, but it was no good. All he could think of was Roe Blaine, and his eyes stayed riveted to the open bedroom doorway.

The world stood still, soundless, with each of these three men hardly daring to breathe. And then, as Lew had guessed it would, Blaine's gun and gun hand poked out past the doorjamb a split second ahead of his body.

Lew's hand flashed to his right hand gun. As it did, Vogel made a dive for his own weapon. Lew's mind thought with lightning rapidity: *He'll have trouble getting it out of the holster.*

His gun came out and up, and the hammer clicked audibly as it came back. Blaine stepped into the room. His eyes flicked instantly to Lew.

From the corner of his eye, Lew saw that Vogel, through freakish luck, had experienced no difficulty with his holstered gun. He had it out and was bringing it to bear.

Death had a cold hand on Lew's shoulder. But something fierce within him would not yet give up. He flung a shot at Blaine's shoulder, knowing even as he did that there would be no time to determine whether or not he scored a hit. The instant his gun bucked in his hand, he swiveled his glance to Vogel.

He saw the flash of Vogel's gun. He felt a searing pain along his ribs and instinctively lurched away from it. He caught his balance almost immediately. This time Vogel, his gun moving with Lew, missed because Lew had stopped. And Blaine, crazed with pain in his shoulder, lurched between the two.

Lew flung his gun. It struck Vogel in the chest and drove him away. Like a panther, Lew was across the room. Viciously he caught Vogel's arm and twisted. Vogel's gun clattered to the floor.

Lew flung the man away from him. He glared at the pair. Blaine was defiant, white-faced with pain. But Vogel cowered like a whipped dog. Lew stooped and picked up his gun.

Vogel babbled frantically: "Lew, it wasn't my idea. I thought Blaine was a cowpuncher. That's what I hired him for. He's the one that wanted to take your old man's place. He told me he'd kill me if I didn't go along."

Lew looked at Blaine. He said: "See what you're working for, Blaine?"

Blaine's voice was weak, but it contained the same disgust his eyes had held. "I'm not working for him any more."

Lew said: "Sit down. I'll look at your shoulder."

Blaine sat down. Lew ripped the underwear away from the shoulder. He grunted: "Missed the bone. Hurts, but you'll be all right." He turned to Vogel. "Fix him up." He watched while Vogel bandaged the shoulder. When the man was finished, Lew said: "You're a little man, Vogel. Stay little. I won't be so damned easy on you next time."

He turned his back and strode out of the house, carefully fingering the bullet burn along his ribs to see how bad it was. Deciding it would wait, he mounted and rode over to the bunched crowd in front of Stirrup's bunkhouse. He said harshly: "Boys, Stirrup has decided not to grow. Get your horses and ride out. Don't come back."

He had no worry that they would not obey. Vogel couldn't hold them together after what had happened, and Blaine was leaving.

Lew rode away with his father following silently behind. He said as they cleared the yard: "I didn't kill either one of them. I nicked Blaine, but I didn't kill him."

Jared Harvey said: "All right, Lew. All right."

Lew said: "I'm going to stay in the Sand Hills. I'm going to marry Nance."

"All right."

Lew drew his horse to a halt. Dawn had grayed the eastern sky, and by its faint light he could see his father's face. The last measure of maturity came then to Lew, and he said: "I was the wrong one, three years ago. I'll try to make it up."

A moment escaped.

Jared Harvey smiled, and years seemed to drop from his tired face. He said: "No need for that. Rake that horse of yours with the spurs. Nance is waiting for you."

Lew Harvey did.

Rustler's Run

In the winter of 1948–1949, in addition to losing his herd of cattle, Lewis B. Patten underwent other hardships. His wife was away from home, nursing her aged step-mother. Patten's son Clifford fell ill with fever. Patten had only an open Jeep that could not be used to transport his son to a Denver hospital where he would receive medical attention. That night he kept the boy in bed with him, and the next day his wife returned in the family car to transport the boy to Denver. When they arrived at the hospital, the doctor met the Pattens on the front steps. After examining the boy, he told his parents that he could not guarantee that he would be able to save him, but fortunately the boy did not die. Among his fictional characters, Patten developed his women as well as the men, and often domestic life was the center of focus, as is certainly the case in "Rustler's Run." It was first published in *Thrilling Ranch Stories* (Spring, 1953) and, as the other short novels in this trio, has never before appeared in book form.

I

"Girl Trouble"

On Saturday morning, Burt loaded four blocks of salt into the panniers of his pack saddle and trailed up onto Riley's Mesa with it. When he got back at eleven, Stella was still in bed. He could hear her light snores from the open door of the bedroom.

With resignation mixed with distaste, he straightened up the house, and washed the dishes. The empty whisky bottle, the one Sam Shirer had brought, he tossed into the coal scuttle. Except for Sam's pursuit of Stella, he did not dislike the man. Yet he distrusted the whisky and hated it for the things it did to her. He distrusted Sam for bringing it, aware that Sam had a purpose in bringing it, this purpose being to weaken the force of Stella's refusal.

When he had the dishes washed, he tossed the pan of soapy water out the door and picked up the broom. He was a tall kid of eighteen, whose face was too sober and brooding for his age, whose eyes held too much habitual bitterness.

Some devil of loneliness rode Stella. When she awoke today, she would be repentant, and for a while would be as good a mother to Burt as it was possible for her to be. She would wash and scrub and, if her remorse did not peter out too soon, would likely bake a dried apple pie. Tomorrow her eyes would again assume the old somber look, and this would grow with the days and the weeks.

Burt set the broom in the corner with a light shrug. His shoulders were thin, lacking flesh but not muscle, wide and sloping. His belly was flat below a good, deep chest. He snatched up a towel and a bar of strong soap, going out the sagging door, down the beaten path to the creek. Here he stripped off his clothes and walked into the water, into the deepest pool that came exactly to his knees.

He squatted and splashed water over himself, then stood while he lathered thoroughly. He kept thinking of the dance tonight at the schoolhouse in Mustang. He'd have his fun for a while, but it would end as it always ended, with cruel taunts that brought on the inevitable fighting in the soft dark behind the old log building.

He wondered briefly why he bothered to go. All he got out of it was the body soreness of too much pounding, skinned knuckles, a split lip, and maybe a black eye. Yet deep within him was a vague awareness that not to go would be some kind of an admission, would be a retreat before Mitch Riorson and his brothers.

He splashed out of the water and dried himself on the gravelly bank, rubbing until the pink showed in his skin. He slipped on his pants and boots, and, carrying shirt and towel, returned toward the house, pausing for an instant at his own sleeping quarters in the bunkhouse for clean shirt and pants. Then he went on.

Stella came out of the bedroom as he entered, her eyes bloodshot, her face slack, her hair a black, gleaming tangle.

Burt said—" 'Mornin', Ma."—and she drew the faded robe closer about her, this being a gesture, a reaction. She would not meet his eyes. Shame rode her this morning, and in Burt stirred a peculiar compassion for her shame. He ought to hate her, and this he had told himself a thousand times. Yet hate is compounded of intolerance and a lack of understanding. She hurt him by her actions. She had made his life a continuing defense of her actions, her drinking. She put defiance and bravado into all of his relations with other people. Even so, he could understand the forces that drove her, and understanding cannot live with intolerance.

Stella had never really recovered from Nick Norden's death. Essentially she was a one-man woman; she had worshipped Nick, Burt's father; she had been one with him in a way that was beautiful and wonderful to see. When they had brought Nick's bullet-ridden body home, sagging across his saddle, her hysteria, her lost and terrible screaming had been something Burt could never forget. Nor was he now able to forget the weeks, the months when Stella had sat in her rocker, face bleak and still from her thoughts, not eating, not sleeping.

Liquor had brought release to Stella, liquor and Sam Shirer, and a couple of others before him, others who had stopped coming when they discovered that not even liquor could overcome Stella's stubborn loyalty to dead Nick Norden. Yet in a small community, a widow, whisky, late hours with a man could spell but one thing. So they talked about Stella, and the talk got back to her son.

Because Burt knew she would not eat unless he fixed a meal and ate with her, he went outside and rummaged about the base of the haystack until he found four eggs. When he came back in, she had combed her hair. He said, as he shaved a stick of kindling into the stove box: "I packed some salt over to Riley's Mesa. The grass is better up there than anywhere else this time of year, but the cattle won't go that far from water unless there's salt to tempt them."

"That's fine, Burt. You cleaned up in here, too." She waited a moment, a moment that dragged and dragged, finally saying in a soft and almost inaudible voice the thing Burt had known she must say: "Burt, I won't do it again."

"I know, Ma. I know you won't."

He sliced bacon from the piece on the table, and laid the strips in the skillet. When the water in the coffee pot boiled, he dropped in a handful of coffee. The smell of bacon and coffee mingled in the room, growing strong and sharp. Stella made her silent fight against nausea, won, and took her place at the table, allowing Burt to serve her with crisp bacon and fried eggs.

Her eyes kept begging him until finally he said: "It's all right, Ma. It's all right. There's a dance tonight. I'm going."

"You taking Lucy?"

He shrugged. "Haven't asked her. I'll ride past there on the way to town. You want anything from the store?"

"I guess not." She looked at Burt in a puzzled way, her still-smooth forehead making a frown. "Burt . . . Burt, I wish you wouldn't go tonight."

"Why?"

"I don't know." She shrugged. "It was a feeling I had. It's gone now."

Burt got up from the table. He changed his pants and put on the clean shirt. Stella smiled, saying: "Go on with you. Have a good time."

He went outside, got his saddle and bridle from the barn, going then to the corral. He took his rope from the saddle and shook out a loop as he went through the corral gate. Dread became suddenly concrete and physical within him. His fights with Mitch Riorson had become more savage as time went on. Although he would not put words to his uneasiness, he knew that the time was not far off when these fights must reach killing intensity.

He swung into his saddle, riding out the four or five stiff-legged jumps the Roman-nosed gray made, then raised a hand to Stella in the doorway. She was a tall and dark-haired woman, whose body showed none of the fullness of approaching middle age. Her face was smooth and unlined. Except for haunted loneliness, her eyes were soft and warm, gray and clear. She was thirty-five, too young not to need a man, but having her standards set high because of Nick Norden it would take a good man to fill Nick's place in Stella's heart. She had not found him yet. Perhaps she never would.

Stella gave him a farewell smile, a smile forced and strained, and left with him the vaguest feeling of unhappiness, a feeling that rode with him all the way to Clevis Cross. Norden's N Bar outfit lay on an upland meadow, traversed by a narrow creek, backed against the steep and darkly timbered slopes of the Virginia Peaks. Before N Bar's meadow lay a drop-off of five hundred feet to the turbulent waters of the Bear. The road rose from the banks of the Bear here, in steep switchbacks, to wind through Norden's meadow before dropping again into the valley that widened like a funnel as it approached the town of Mustang.

All along this road, and all the roads of this country, the slopes were dotted with the brown scars of mine dumps. In earlier times, the valley of the Bear had been mining country, until the richest of the veins had petered out, until transportation became a thing that took the profit out of the remaining low-grade ores.

Halfway to town, another road bridged the river to disappear into the timber, and it was this turning that Burt took. It wound upward, over a high ridge, to descend into the wide valley of Clevis Cross and of the Riorsons' Rocking R on the other side.

In late afternoon sunlight, the strong and pungent odors of pine resins became a solid and pleasant thing in the still air. The rustlings along the trail were nearly continuous as wild creatures scurried away from the sound of approaching hoofs.

Below, as the timber thinned, Burt could see the buildings of Clevis Cross, scattered in haphazard fashion through the short meadow grass. A new haystack, not yet darkened by sun and rain, stood, green and fresh, beside the big log barn. Above, in haze-shrouded distance, a sawmill whined, the sawmill of the Riorsons, and there a blue cloud of smoke rose.

Riding through the yard, Burt nodded at the two 'punchers, patiently working a frightened bay colt, and dismounted beside the long, screened porch that opened into the kitchen. A shaggy dog came from beneath this porch, his tail a-wag, and sniffed at Burt's legs in friendly fashion, begging abjectly with his eyes for a pat on the head. Burt reached down and scratched his ears, calling through the screening: "Hey! Anybody home?"

"Come in, Burt." It was a girl's voice, careful and without expression.

He went in, finding Lucy ironing a dress at the long kitchen table. Shyness touched him and a consciousness of his gangling awkwardness. This was the way between them now, she pink-faced, he clumsy and tongue-tied. He grunted: "Dance tonight. Want to go?"

She faced him, putting aside her iron, a small and fair-haired girl of sixteen, delicately rounded, her full lips compressed, her smooth face turning pale with resentment. "You! Do you think I'll sit here and hold my breath waiting for you to get around to asking me to the dance? I'll have you know there are lots of boys who'd like to take me. I'll have you know that I can go with any boy I want!" She tossed her shoulder-length blonde hair so that it brushed her cheeks, high-colored with defiance.

Her outburst startled and puzzled him. For an instant he stammered, then said the first thing that came into his head:

"What's eatin' you? You ain't never had to be asked ahead of time before."

"Well, I do now. I'm going with Mitch Riorson. He asked me yesterday. I guess he likes me as well as you do, and he knows how to treat a girl."

Burt felt the flush of anger rising to his face. Awkwardness was suddenly gone from him. Beneath the unreasonable stirring of anger was a deep and bitter disappointment. Theirs had been a boy and girl relationship, very casual, very undemanding. Always, when he had come to see her, her welcome had been matter-of-fact, with none of this unfathomed perversity to complicate it.

He guessed the change had come about less than a week past, that dark, rainy day, Monday. Riding together at the head of Clevis Cross's meadow, caught by a sudden squall, they had left their horses and run to the shelter of a tiny one-room cabin. Laughing, drenched, Lucy in his arms, they kissed, her cold face snuggling against his neck afterward. Remembrance gave him delicious shivers whenever he thought of it.

Now he was discovering that Monday had been the end of something, the end of easy camaraderie, the beginning of something else. He asked: "You mad at me for Monday?"

Her stare was long and level, showing none of her thoughts, only the plain hostility generated by them. Her voice became tight and small. "Why should I be mad? Why should I?" Only her eyes cried out: *You didn't need to wait a whole week! You could have come back! Didn't it mean anything to you at all? You've spoiled it! You've spoiled it!*

Burt wanted to plead with her, yet pride became stiff-backed and would not let him. He said darkly: "You want to watch out for that Mitch Riorson. You want to watch out for him, that's all."

He whirled and tramped through the door. On the porch steps he stumbled, recovered himself with burning cheeks, and mounted with considerably more haste than skill.

The startled gray bolted, yet recklessness and anger would not permit Burt to check him, and so he went away at a hard run, seething with still another reason for fighting Mitch Riorson tonight, not caring now how bitter or intense the fighting might become, nor how hurt he might get.

II

"Too Many Riorsons"

Down the long valley, the valley that wound its narrowing way a full fifteen miles above the Riorsons' sawmill, came John Cross in late afternoon, grim of face, followed by eight silent and grim-faced Clevis 'punchers. At the Riorsons' fence he dismounted, and held the wire gate, scowling as his men rode through, then refastening it and mounting.

Seeing them, Dan Riorson, heavy and thick, came hurrying down the road to intercept them as they passed his house. "Well, John?"

"Nothing! Not a damned thing! Tally shows eighteen more head gone and not a trace to show where. I had men at the pass, men on this road. Today we rode Timberline Ridge looking for tracks. Elk tracks aplenty, but no cattle tracks, or horse tracks, either. Somebody's getting cattle out of here. I'm out over two hundred since the first of the year. Pitchfork below me has lost over a hundred. Guiry's lost as many as I have. Somebody's getting rich." Turned irritable by failure, he suddenly asked: "How many you lost, Riorson?"

Dan Riorson, whose broad Irish face had heretofore held a secret glint of amusement, suddenly stepped forward, laying a heavy hand on Cross's bridle. "You mean anything special by that question, John?" There was dull anger in the red of his face, truculence in the set of his jaw.

Cross felt moved to temper the veiled accusation that had been in his remark, yet some new stubbornness sealed his lips.

Impatience stirred him, and suddenly Dan Riorson became an object on which he could vent his frustration. Spurs in his horse's sides sent the animal lunging forward, against the restraining hand of Dan Riorson. Riorson was solid, thick. He held on. The horse reared, striking with his fore hoofs. One of them struck Riorson's shoulder, and knocked him sprawling. Cross held his horse still with a heavy hand, facing the irate Irishman as he rose to his knees. He felt a sudden regret for this, yet there was no apology in him, no retreat. He said: "Keep your damned hands off till you're ready for a fight, Dan."

Riorson's eyes glittered. He stood, spraddle-legged, heavy and squat and dangerous. A gun sat fat and ready at his solid thigh, yet he made no move toward it. He growled: "Eight men at your back. Try me when you're alone sometime, John."

"I'll do that." Cross's sense of wrongness was on the increase, but the devil of stubbornness remained. Without further talk, he reined around and went down the road at a gallop, his eight 'punchers close-packed behind.

At five, he came into the yard at Clevis Cross and swung off his horse, handing up the reins to Dorian, the foreman. He stalked to the house to find Lucy, her light hair in curlers, basting a steaming beef roast resting on the oven door.

It was with an obvious effort that John Cross controlled his irritability. He grunted: "Hmm. Dance tonight, eh?"

Lucy nodded, rising and smiling, yet there was no happiness, no anticipation in this smile.

"Who are you going with, that Norden kid?"

"No. Mitch Riorson."

It brought him around, irritability forgotten in the rise of surprise and uneasiness. He had interfered little in Lucy's life since she had assumed care of the house at Clevis Cross, feeling that if she was mature enough for this, she was mature enough to order her own life without interference. He had not missed the talk about Stella Norden. He had known that eventually talk that touched Stella and Burt must touch Lucy, too, if she continued to see Burt. Yet his opposition to Burt had been passive, made thus by his instinctive liking for the boy. He had hoped for another young man in Lucy's life, another to give Burt competition.

Finding that it was Mitch Riorson suddenly moved him to anger. He said: "Stay away from him. He's the meanest of that whole damned clan. There ain't a horse on Riorson's place that won't roll his eyes and back off when Mitch comes near him." He saw the rise of defiance in Lucy, and with unexpected wisdom changed the subject. "How's your ma?"

"The same. She coughs a lot."

"I'll go see her." Turned vaguely unhappy by Lucy's date with Mitch, filled with helplessness in the face of slow and steady rustling of his cattle, he went out of the kitchen and climbed the creaking stairs to Mrs. Cross's room.

She lay passively in the middle of the big, four-poster bed, pale and thin, gaunt of face, hollow of eye. He said, his voice gentle: "Faith, how you feeling?"

"All right." Her smile was apologetic. "I'll get up tomorrow. This big house is too much for a girl."

He nodded. "For a little while, if you want." He sat down beside her on the bed, a big and red-faced man, full of man's unreasonableness and occasional savagery, but moved to gentleness in the presence of this frail woman who was so familiar to him. She would not get up tomorrow, or any tomorrow, he admitted to himself. This was simply a ritual that she went through with him, only for the purpose of letting him know she had not given up hope.

He bent and kissed her forehead. *How long?* he wondered. *How long?*

She asked: "How is the work going, John?"

"Fine. Fine." He had kept this rustling business from her, this rustling that had no apparent solution and that had kept getting steadily worse since it started something over a year ago. There seemed little point in adding another worry to those she already bore.

Now she asked, her voice turned weak: "Lucy's going with Burt?"

For an instant John Cross's face darkened. Then he shrugged. "Who else?" he evaded.

"He's a good boy. His mother is a fine woman. How is she standing the loss of her husband, John?"

She reminded John suddenly by her talk how long she had been bed-ridden. She did not know then how Stella had stood the loss of Nick Norden. Her visitors, knowing her attachment to Stella Norden, had never mentioned the gossip concerning Stella in her presence. Again, John evaded: "She still grieves."

"I'll get up tomorrow and go visit her."

"All right." He never argued with Faith. Tomorrow she would swing her legs over the side of the bed with full intentions of getting up. But weakness would claim her before she could stand, and she would murmur: "I am weak today. I'll do it tomorrow."

He smoothed her forehead tenderly with his hand, finding it feverish and damp. "Go to sleep," he murmured. "I'll bring you something to eat after Lucy's gone."

Faith nodded and smiled. John Cross went from the room, saddened and depressed.

During dinner he was grim and silent. His mind wrestled futilely with the mystery of the vanishing cattle, settling finally upon the touchiness of Dan Riorson as the one slight opening in the blank wall of his puzzlement. Lucy finished before him and went to her room to prepare for the dance. As he was finishing his coffee, he heard hoofs in the yard, and went to the door.

Mitch Riorson tied his buckboard team to a tree and strode toward him, squat and heavy as was Dan Riorson, his father, heavy of brow and lip. Mitch made a smile, showing large, white teeth as his lips split away from them. It was Mitch's eyes that bothered John Cross the most. Narrow-lidded and narrow-set in his broad face, they were entirely without warmth. Mitch Riorson occasionally could smile with his heavy lips. John Cross had never seen his smile extend to his eyes. Mitch was eighteen. He carried a gun, and he carried a knife, not being particularly skillful with either. Fists were Mitch Riorson's long suit—and knees and elbows and feet. These were the things he had used on his brothers during the eighteen years of his life, and he had become expert with them.

Mitch asked: "Lucy ready?"

"Not quite." Cross hesitated a moment, saying finally: "I damned near made an issue of this tonight. I'm surprised Dan didn't, after the jangle I had with him this afternoon." He felt his anger rise and his voice with it and found himself powerless to stop. He said: "You be careful. You be damned careful, or I'll take it out of your hide. You understand?"

"Ahh. . . ." Cross never knew what Mitch might have said, for he heard Lucy's step on the porch behind him. Her face was still and unsmiling. She planted a dutiful peck on John Cross's cheek and stepped lightly toward the buckboard. The horses laid back their ears as Mitch took up the reins.

Cross called—"Drive like you had some sense."—and knew the instant he uttered it that the admonition was futile. At a fast trot the horses went out of the meadow and, where the road entered the timber, broke into a run.

John Cross cursed, and slammed the door with unaccustomed violence as he rëentered the house.

III

"Murder Will Out"

Only stubbornness kept Burt Norden pointed toward town after he left Clevis Cross that afternoon—stubbornness, anger, and the fixed notion that he should be on hand to see that nothing happened to Lucy in Mitch Riorson's company.

The town of Mustang lay at the point where Bear River entered the deep, dark, and narrow cañon for its racing, plunging passage to the plain. No roads or trails traversed that deep cleft in naked rock, and only the river passed through it, narrowed to fifty feet in places, dropping so swiftly between the sheer towering walls that it assumed an incredible speed. Nothing, in the memory of man, had ever passed down that cañon and lived. Horses occasionally were swept into it, to emerge a short hour later on the plain, battered and lifeless. A man had once tried it in a boat, and broken bits of the boat were all that were ever found.

Half of Mustang laid on one side of the river, joined to the other half by a stout, timber bridge. The entrance to the cañon was a short quarter mile from the bridge, and on most nights the roar of cascading water in the cañon was clearly audible in the town. The road out of Mustang wound upward across a high ridge, dropping then in gradual stages through heavy timber, to emerge on the plain twenty miles and countless switchbacks later.

Burt dismounted at the big livery barn, and led his horse inside. He off-saddled and rubbed the gray's back briefly with a sack. Then he led the animal outside, watered him, and was forking hay to the horse when the hostler, Jed Priest, came from the pool hall and stopped to watch.

"In for the dance, kid?"

Burt nodded, fished in his pocket for a quarter, and handed the money to Priest.

"Where's your gal?"

A frail attempt at defense made Burt say defiantly: "Who?"

"Why, Lucy Cross. Who else?"

"She's coming with Mitch."

"Had a spat, huh?"

Anger spilled over in Burt at Jed's gentle prying. Angry words rose in his throat, but he stifled them, for in Jed's seamed features there was only friendliness. Jed had a strong and gamy smell, the smell of horses and sweat, of manure and beer and garlic. His eyes were bright blue, now showing considerable understanding. "You just come for the fight then, I reckon."

Burt was silent, wanting to get away, made uncomfortable by Jed's persistence. Jed said: "Watch Mitch, son. Watch them sneaky brothers of his. Don't ever let 'em rig you into a fight anywheres but there at the dance where there's other people around to see you get a fair shake."

"I guess I can look out for myself."

Jed shrugged. "Mebbe. Mebbe not. I see the way Riorson horses act around Mitch. They're an ornery outfit, boy, and don't you forget it, from the old man on down. But Mitch is the worst." He seemed to drop the subject of Mitch as abruptly as he had taken it up, saying then: "You been losin' cattle?"

"I'm out five. Strayed over Timberline Ridge onto Cross's range, I reckon. I got to get over there and hunt for them . . . tomorrow maybe."

Jed grinned. "Funny thing. The only ones losin' cattle is them that runs with Clevis Cross above the Riorsons' place. What you want to bet you never see them five again?"

Burt frowned. "You think . . . ?"

Jed interrupted hastily: "I don't think a damned thing! It ain't safe to think in this country." He seemed suddenly to lose interest in Burt. Turning, he fished a plug of tobacco from his pocket and bit off a piece. He picked up a fork and began to clean a stall.

Burt hesitated a moment, then turned uncertainly, heading out of the stable and toward town. For no tangible reason, his thoughts turned to his father. Nick Norden had been found on Clevis Cross range. His errand in that long valley had been to locate strays. When he did not return, Burt had gone to look for him, well knowing that a horse can fall, a man can be thrown, any of a dozen accidents can happen to a lone rider. He had been prepared to find his father hurt. He had not been prepared to find him dead, shot half a dozen times with a high-powered rifle.

The nightmare of that day was etched permanently on his brain, having even now the power to turn him cold with horror. Again he experienced the terrible sense of loss he had known that day, followed by a boy's tortured grief and helplessness, and the inevitable need for revenge, to kill the killer of his father.

More than a year had passed since then. The sheriff, over special from the county seat, had spent a week at Mustang and riding the countryside. It had been a futile thing. The sheriff had found no clues, had been unable to uncover a motive. Nick Norden, big and good-natured, had been well-liked throughout the country. Why should anyone want to kill him? Why? Burt was certain that, when he could answer that question, he could also name the killer.

Yet time has its way of slipping past. Burt could not forever ride the country searching for a shadow. With Nick gone, the running of the ranch fell upon his inexperienced shoulders. There was hay to put up, salt to pack, endless riding to be done. There were fences to be fixed, chores to be done twice daily. These things kept a steady ache in Burt's stringy body, kept his brain dull with fatigue, gave him no time to puzzle over the insoluble problem of his father's murder.

Life went on. Stella brooded and grew bitter; she turned to liquor and seemed unable to stop herself. Eventually she would become what the country already accused her of being. The memory of Nick Norden faded in Burt, as time fades all memories.

Yet someday, and of this Burt was sure, someone would turn a stone and under it would lie the answer. John Cross had put the words to it: "Murder will out." It was for this that Burt waited, but the waiting seemed endless.

He headed through the deep dust in the street for the pool hall, the hot afternoon sun against his back making welcome the thought of the cool, half dark of the place, the idle click of ball against ball. There was time to be passed before it would be late enough for the dance to begin. There was no place in town where a boy might spend this time save for the pool hall.

Beneath the board awning of Gundersen's Grocery, he met Mrs. Gundersen, who had just come from the door, broom in hand, to sweep off the walk. Burt touched the brim of his hat, saying: "Howdy, ma'am."

Her attention came around to him, with the faintest thinning of her lips, the slightest hardening of her eyes. Because she was a businesswoman, and because the Nordens had always traded with her, she forced from herself the grudging smile that never hid her disapproval, but only seemed to accentuate it. "Hello, Burt."

Her glance held him still for a moment, fidgeting uneasily. Perhaps with some thought for the unpaid balance of the Nordens' account, waiting shipping time for settlement, she asked carefully: "How are you folks making out? Are you losing cattle?"

He repeated stolidly for her what he had told Jed Priest. "I'm only out five, ma'am. Strayed, I reckon. I'll ride over to Clevis Cross tomorrow to hunt for them."

He went on to the pool hall, finding it nearly empty. Idly he chose a cue and racked the balls. The click of balls became a somnolent sound, and gradually he became preoccupied with the satisfaction of his shots, which were skillful and precise. Unnoticed, the sun dropped against the timbered horizon and sank from sight. Coolness flowed down the slopes like water. Wind drifted townward from the gorge, bringing the roaring noise of the plunging river, making a sort of ominous murmur that became a background for the sharper street noises.

Wagons bearing the ranch owners, their wives and children, began rolling into the town. Almost to a man, they drew up before the hotel to discharge their passengers, then rumbled downstreet to the livery barn. Cowpunchers came horseback, freshly shaved, scrubbed until they shone, wearing their best and with their hair slicked down with grease.

Mitch Riorson drove the Riorson buckboard in, and beside him Lucy's face was white and scared. Mitch's team was heavily lathered from running, and upon their wet backs were the fresh marks of his whip. He drew up before the hotel as Burt came from the pool hall, and Burt paused there, watching as Lucy jumped lightly down and went up the hotel steps. Mitch Riorson howled and laid the whip across the backs of his team.

Burt became suddenly conscious of the grinning stares from the loungers' bench, and from behind him came some coolly insolent remark that he failed to catch, but that drew a shout of ribald laughter. Flushing and reckless, Burt swung around, his eyes seeking vainly for the one who had spoken. With no thought for the ridiculousness of this he said sharply—"What?"—and, when he got no answer: "If anybody has got anything to say, just step out and say it real plain so's I can hear."

He had expected nothing but the abashed and downcast eyes, the occasional conciliatory grin. A man at the end murmured: "We kid a lot, Burt, but there ain't no thorns in it."

Another said: "I'll put five to three on Burt tonight."

Suddenly angry, Burt stalked away, following the street toward the saloons at its lower end. Ho's Restaurant stopped him, with its smells of frying meat, and hungry with youth's ravenousness he turned into it. The only empty stool was beside curly-haired Pete Guiry, a year older than Burt, from the Guiry spread below Clevis Cross. Burt sat down and gave his order for steak and spuds to the gleaming-faced Chinaman. He muttered: "Hello, Pete. You in for the dance?"

"You bet. Burt, I got a bottle stashed in the weeds back of the schoolhouse. You see me tonight."

Burt nodded sociably, but without any intention of complying. This was the way it was. The women of the community would allow no drinking within the confines of the schoolhouse. Yet beside each fencepost was a bottle, behind every clump of brush.

In early evening, the dance progressed with vaguely uncomfortable amiability until the cached liquor began to take effect. Then all of the hidden and secret animosities exploded to find expression in the solid thump of fist on flesh. A good many of the more prominent families would leave before that time. Most of the young ones would stay on, the Riorsons, Pete Guiry, Burt, a dozen others.

Burt thought of Lucy, of her white-faced fright. He began to anticipate the inevitable meeting with Mitch; he began to feel a heady and rising recklessness. He knew that Mitch would take the trip to Pete Guiry's bottle often tonight, and would grow more savage with each trip. He knew with abrupt surety that he must somehow take Lucy home himself. If he whipped Mitch tonight, Mitch would take his surly resentment out on Lucy and on his buckboard team. If Mitch whipped him, it would be much the same, except that Mitch's prod would be the intoxication of victory. Either way Lucy would be subjected not only to fright at the way Mitch drove, but to real danger as well.

Burt realized he was shaking, and again felt the odd premonition that had bothered him earlier today. For no tangible reason, he thought of Stella's words: "It was a feeling I had. It's gone now."

Inevitably he knew and had thought of it, that if the fighting with blocky and savage Mitch Riorson continued, a time would come when animosity and hatred reached killing intensity. Perhaps that time was tonight. Sweating lightly, Burt paid for his meal and rose. With his young face grim, he walked purposefully toward the schoolhouse.

IV

"Fight to the Finish"

The schoolhouse at Mustang was a large, log building with but a single room inside. For this occasion, desks had been shoved all to one side and sat there in a triple row against the wall, providing seats for the onlookers, for those who would rather watch than participate. Lanterns hung from a beam down the center of the room, ten in all, and at one end was a raised platform holding a piano and half a dozen straight-backed chairs. In one of these sat frail and hunchbacked Kenny Boorom, drawing bow across fiddle strings, tuning up. A polite crowd of womenfolk clustered about the long table on the opposite wall from the bunched desks, stirring and sampling the punch. Beside the door, as Burt entered, he heard old man Guiry mutter: "A man ought to spike that punch a bit. I'll tell you, boys, walk up there with me and crowd the womenfolks aside, and I'll dump this bottle I've got."

A guffaw answered his suggestion, and the crowd of them moved away, chuckling, for all the world like a bunch of boys anticipating a prank. One of them whispered: "Them women'll have a better time tonight than they've ever had, an' they won't know why."

Burt looked around, found Lucy sitting demurely at one of the desks, Mitch Riorson surly and red-faced beside her. As he watched, Pete Guiry came in, going directly to Mitch, and after a short discussion the two moved across the floor and out the door.

Lucy sent a look toward Burt that was fear-filled and beseeching. He went over, saying nothing, and the red came into her face before she murmured: "Could you manage to take me home tonight, Burt? He scares me. He drives like crazy."

"All right. I'll go down to the stable and hire a rig." Strangeness lay between them, turning Lucy shy, making Burt uncomfortably warm. He turned to go, but she rose, laid a small hand on his arm. "Burt, I'm sorry. I'll slip outside and wait. Then you won't have to fight him."

He stiffened. "I guess I can handle him. You stay here. I won't go sneaking away, and you hadn't ought to ask me to."

He saw the rise and fall of protest in her, and, with her standing wordless, he turned away. He went directly downstreet to the stable, and came back twenty minutes later driving a hired buckboard that he tied in a clump of trees a hundred yards from the schoolhouse. As he entered, the piano began to bang, the fiddler broke into a lively tune. Mitch swaggered to Lucy and yanked her to her feet. Burt took a step forward, then forced himself to halt. *Not yet . . . not yet.*

The dance gained momentum. Sweat began to glisten on the men's foreheads. Jed Priest, hair slicked down but otherwise unchanged, called the dance in his high and penetrating voice.

Fingers tugged at Burt's sleeve, and Pete Guiry murmured: "Come on. You ain't tried my jug yet."

Killing his reluctance, Burt followed outside into the soft and velvet darkness. Pete found the bottle, uncorked it, and offered it to Burt. It was half empty. Pete said softly: "You better watch Mitch tonight, Burt. He left his gun in the buckboard, but he's carrying his knife. He's getting lit and turning mean. He's bragging that he'll cut your liver out."

Burt choked on the liquor, going into a spasm of coughing. He gasped, spluttered, and Pete Guiry laughed. “Too strong, huh?” He took the bottle from Burt, drank, and manfully controlled his involuntary shudder.

Warmth began to grow in Burt’s stomach, and an odd and overpowering feeling of well-being. He had a fleeting feeling that tonight all things might be possible. For no particular reason, he thought of the five strays he was missing. He said: “Your outfit runs with Clevis Cross. You see anything of five of mine up there lately?”

Pete corked the bottle and put it carefully away. “No. John Cross rode this week. Pa and me rode the week before. We didn’t see none of yours.” He stood up, and moved slowly toward the lights. He said in a puzzled voice: “We’re out two hundred since the first of the year. How the hell do they get ’em out of there? They don’t bring ’em past our place. They don’t bring ’em through Clevis Cross. The only other way out of there is over Timberline Ridge, or over the pass, and we’ve had men watching for that.”

“How many’re the Riorsons missing?”

“Dan says forty. Pa doubted it and made a rough check. Looks like the truth.”

They approached the schoolhouse, and old man Guiry’s deep voice came from the crowd. “Hell, I’ll put a man to watchin’ every damned critter I’ve got if I have to. I’ll stop it. I tell you, I’ll stop it some way.”

Agatha Guiry appeared in the lighted doorway, calling sharply into the darkness: “Roy! Roy, you come in.”

Pete went up the steps after his father, and Burt followed, still with the unaccustomed warmth in the pit of his stomach. He stood in the light crowd at the door, watching the dance, and out of the press of bodies somewhere came Mitch Riorson’s deliberate taunt: “I ain’t seen Sam Shirer tonight.

Now where you reckon he could be?"

Burt thought: *Here it is.* Tension came to all his muscles and a tight, choked feeling to his throat. He was not afraid of Mitch, he told himself, yet he could feel his face paling. Mitch shoved through the crowd, which had now assumed an expectant quiet. A soft voice beside Burt murmured: "Don't you mind, boy. Don't pay no heed to him."

Mitch stopped before him, truculent and palely vicious. "I'll make it plainer. Sam won't get back to town till morning. You started callin' him pa yet, Burt?"

Burt's fist swung wildly out, catching Mitch squarely on his flat, flaring nose. Blood ran redly across Mitch's face. A man yelled: "Here! None of that in here! Take it outside, boys."

But Burt had followed his attack. With flailing fists he now drove Mitch back into the press of bodies. They gave way before him, and Mitch went sprawling on the smooth dance floor. Burt sought to leap upon him, but hands caught at him, held him away. Mitch got to his feet, narrow-eyed, grinning wicked anticipation. "Sure," he said. "Let's take it outside."

Somewhere Burt could hear Lucy's soft crying. A way opened to the door, and around Mitch and Burt closed the bodies of the men. Behind them arose sharp voices of outrage from the women. "Every time!" one said. And another: "That Norden woman! Why don't she . . . ?"

"The boy's as bad. Fighting . . . drinking . . . heaven knows what all. I'd never let my girl go around with him, I can tell you that."

Burt felt the steps under his feet, then the hard-packed dirt of the schoolyard. He heard Mitch's throaty chuckle not far away. He moved with the crowd and presently found himself within a small circle. At one side of this circle stood a man with a lantern. Mitch half crouched across from him, grinning in his evil way. Out in the darkness a voice cried: "Fight! Fight! Hurry up!"

Mitch said—"All right."—and came forward, a little bow-legged, a little crouched. Burt swung forward with a rush. His fist went out, smashed the thatch of Mitch's hair and his solid skull beneath, as Mitch ducked his head. Pain shot clear to Burt's elbow. He backed off, and now Mitch straightened, bringing a ponderous fist upward in an arc that ended in Burt's groin. A murmur of protest rose from the crowd, and a voice counseled: "Fight him his way. Dirty."

Belly-sickness and nausea flooded Burt. His head reeled with dizziness, and bright, swimming spots danced before his eyes. Instinctively he retreated, waiting for this to pass. Mitch was a blurred, advancing shape before his eyes. As he backed, a foot protruded from the rim of the circle, tripped him, and he went backward helplessly, feeling the shock of the ground suddenly at his back.

A growl of triumph rumbled in Mitch's throat. He came forward at a lumbering run and, when he was yet a yard from Burt, launched himself, feet first, in a clumsy, but effective jump.

His big feet, with his weight behind them, landing in Burt's belly, would have ended the fight once and for all, there then remaining only the pounding against ineffective resistance that would reduce Burt's face to a swollen pulp. But Burt rolled, at the same time raising his legs, so that Mitch's feet came against his hip, found uneven, shifting footing, and slipped away. Mitch tumbled forward, landing beside Burt, and Burt's elbow went out, burying itself in Mitch's groin.

There was an instant's advantage here for Burt, and he took it, surging to his feet. Mitch was also rising, but as Burt came erect, Mitch was only as far as his knees. A moment ago,

Burt would have stepped away and allowed Mitch to rise, for the memory of Mitch's dirty fighting in the past had dimmed. Yet now rage had possessed Burt and a savagery that faintly surprised him. Automatically, with no conscious prompting, his knee came up, swiftly vicious, and slammed with a loudly audible crack against the point of Mitch's jaw.

Mitch's eyes glazed instantly, and his thick-lipped mouth went slack and loose. Burt's fist, in a roundhouse swing, came whistling against the side of Mitch's head, high against his ear, and threw him sideways, off his knees and flat in the dust. Following this advantage, Burt leaped down, white and shaking with fury.

His fists made their short, powerful swings, smashing Mitch's lips, his nose, his eyes. Mitch rolled and raised his hands ineffectively. A snarling curse escaped him. One of his hands, his right, he pulled away from his defense, put it back of him, under him.

Faintly Burt heard the yell: "He's goin' for his knife! Watch him!"

This was the fear in Burt, not of fists and knees, but of sharp, cold steel. Something cold spread outward from his stomach with its paralyzing effect, and helplessly he saw Mitch's right hand come clear with the eight-inch blade. A yell—"Get his hand, kid! Grab it!"—came from the crowd, came dimly through the roaring in Burt's ears.

Mitch was trying to roll, still pinned to the ground by Burt's weight, and, when he found he could not, brought the knife hand sweeping upward in an awkward thrust. The knife found resistance in Burt's thigh, bit into it with its instantaneous, burning pain, and blood flooded from the gash.

Suddenly the rage Burt had experienced before was nothing. New fury soared through him, obliterating all pain, all feeling, all thought. He rolled away from the biting blade, a forearm flung across Mitch's neck to provide leverage.

Mitch choked from the force of Burt's arm against his windpipe, but Burt did not release this pressure even as he felt relief from the cutting edge of the knife. He held his weight this way, against Mitch's throat, while his other hand groped for Mitch's knife wrist, finding instead the blade, which cut his hand, but shifting instantly upward to the wrist, and holding there. There was less strength in Burt's left arm than in Mitch's right, and it was all he could do to hold the knife away from him. Yet he did this, straining his weary and sweating body to its utmost, and gradually, slowly he felt Mitch weaken from lack of air. Convulsively Burt twisted his adversary's knife hand, and thought he felt the knife loosen and slip into the dust.

Mitch, fighting for his breath and his life, made a last, spasmodic effort to free himself, bringing both hands upward to force their strength against Burt's choking weight. His right clawed against Burt, free of the deadly knife, and with this worry suddenly gone, Burt was able to put his full attention, his full strength to depriving the weakened Mitch of air.

Mitch's struggles grew weaker. His face turned dark, and huge veins stood out darkly purple against the deep red of his face. White appeared about his mouth and nostrils, which were pinched and thin as they sucked vainly at the tepid air. Suddenly Mitch's body went slack and loose, yet Burt did not release his hold, fearing another of Mitch's deadly tricks and caught up with a hitherto unsuspected animalistic savagery.

It was hands from above that pulled him away, rough and urgent hands, and voices that cried with quick fear: "Hell, kid, don't kill him!"

Burt released Mitch, allowed himself to be pulled erect. Reaction came. He thought his knees would not support him, and he trembled violently. A man, kneeling over Mitch, rose up, saying: "He's breathing now. He'll be all right."

Burt found himself leaning heavily against Pete Guiry, who pushed the bottle into his hand and said: "One drink left. You need it worse than me." Burt tilted it up, still gasping for air. The fiery stuff choked him, but it went down.

His leg was warm and wet, and Pete Guiry said: "He opened you up like a sack of wheat. Come on, we'll find the doc. Can you walk?"

Burt took an experimental step, then nodded. He let Pete lead him through the awed and shocked crowd of men into the soft and anonymous dark outside the circle.

It was painful to walk—it was painful to think, because he had settled nothing tonight. All he had done was to plant determination in Mitch Riorson—determination to kill.

V

"Last Request"

Old Doc Brady took nine wide-spaced stitches in the gaping thigh wound, and wound a bandage about Burt's leg afterward, saying: "You'll have a nice white scar there as long as you live. You better stay out of trouble with that Riorson outfit, kid, or next time it might not be so easy for me to patch you up."

Sweating and pale, Burt resented the advice, even as he admitted its wisdom. How could he stay out of these fights with Mitch? By ignoring Mitch's taunting slurs? That would keep him out of nothing, for Mitch would simply sharpen the goad and, if even this failed, would carry the fight to Burt himself. There was be no avoiding a fight that someone forced upon you; avoidance only convinced your antagonist that you were afraid.

Burt shrugged weakly, saying: "Pete, will you go and fetch Lucy and the buckboard I hired to take her home? I think I can drive all right, but I'm damned if I feel like walking."

"Sure, Burt." He hesitated at the door for a moment, finally voicing his thoughts reluctantly. "You showed him you could whip his fists and his knife. He'll try his gun on you next."

Burt shrugged, and Pete went off into the darkness. Doc Brady murmured softly: "The sheriff being over in the county seat at Monroe doesn't help any. Mustang ought to have a marshal. It's not good for a town when its law is forty miles away."

Doc was not a big man. He was no larger, no heavier than Burt. He had a dry and caustic wit, yet behind those sharp eyes with their faintly cynical expression was considerable wisdom and a world of kindness. The kids, growing up in Mustang, called him old. Yet "old" Doc was not yet forty. Doc had seen much of human frailty, and out of his experience came a vast tolerance for it, even unsurpassed by Mustang's kindly minister. He asked now: "How's your mother, Burt? It has been too long since I've seen her."

Burt was aware that Doc Brady could not have missed the talk that went around. A doctor heard things as soon as anyone. He said: "She's all right."

Something must have sounded in his voice, some unconcealed resentment, for Doc said: "Don't be too hard on her, son. Your father's death was a terrible shock for her. They were so close. Do not believe the things that are said of her. Folks in a small community live by a pattern, and when someone does not follow the pattern. . . ." Doc Brady hesitated, considered a moment, then said: "Your mother has nothing to do with your fights with Mitch Riorson. It is only the excuse he uses. There's more behind it . . . take my word for it . . . some buried antagonism. Somewhere along the line you must have done something, something you may have forgotten entirely, to earn Mitch's animosity."

Burt considered this briefly, but the pain in his leg throbbed steadily and without let up, and made thinking impossible. Pain such as this had its way of turning him nervous and irritable. He said: "Doc, thanks. Hiring the rig to take Lucy home took all the money I had. I'll be in to see you Saturday."

Doc shrugged. "Any time."

Burt got up, testing his weight against the leg experimentally. He winced. Pete Guiry's feet pounded on the steps, taking them two at a time. He burst into the room. "Burt, I got Lucy outside. Make it quick, will you. I could hear Mitch yellin' for her as I drove away. You ought to get out of town ahead of him so's. . . ." Guiry stopped, then went on, staring at Doc defiantly: "Well, he's got a gun."

Burt hobbled to the door, then stiffened his back and walked down the stairs, with Pete Guiry following worriedly.

Lucy was a still and stiff-backed shape on the buckboard seat, her face white and unsmiling. Tears glistened in her eyes as Burt climbed painfully up beside her. Upstreet, toward the schoolhouse, Mitch Riorson's bellow was muffled and indistinct. Pete Guiry handed up the reins, saying: "Hurry. I'll keep him here fifteen minutes if I have to fight him myself."

Burt nodded, slapped the backs of the team with his reins, and whirled up the valley road toward Clevis Cross. He wished suddenly that he'd had the sense to bring a gun, and, because he could not admit, even to himself, that he was running away, he kept the horses at a slow trot in spite of Lucy's urging.

He knew there was apology in Lucy, knew there was pride as well. Like two strangers they covered the entire distance to Clevis Cross, with only polite, brief comments to break the silence.

Lucy got down with her faint—"Thank you, Burt."—hesitated and seemed about to say something more. Then, leaving it unsaid, she turned and ran toward the house. Burt could never be sure, but he thought he heard Lucy crying just before the big door slammed.

For a while after Lucy left in the buckboard with Mitch, John Cross sat in his big, leather-covered chair before the fireplace, his face angry and darkly brooding. Finally, remembering his wife, bedridden and waiting for her supper upstairs, he went into the kitchen, carved a couple of slices from the beef roast, warmed up the gravy, and made up a plate of supper. Carrying this, he went carefully up the dark stairs. At her door he knocked gently and, when she bid him enter, opened it and went into her room.

The room was in darkness, but long familiarity told John Cross where each piece of furniture was. He set the tray on the dresser, wiped a match alight on the underside of a half-open drawer, and lighted the lamp. Turning toward the bed, he found Faith flushed, her eyes holding that peculiar fever brightness. He watched Faith compassionately. Gone now was the lovely coloring of the girl he had wed, and with whom he had shared the first joys and sorrows of his manhood. He was left with only the memory of her loveliness, and his helpless sorrow for her suffering.

She turned on her side to cough, then smiled apologetically at John as he set the tray before her. "It looks very good, dear. But I am afraid I'll disappoint you. I haven't much appetite lately."

"You need to eat." John's voice was gruff.

"I'll try."

She toyed with the food, obviously preoccupied with her thoughts. John watched her covertly, worriedly. Finally she murmured: "John, go over tomorrow and see Stella for me."

"Why?"

Her added color puzzled him, as did her unaccustomed hesitancy. "Well, I would like to go myself, but I'm afraid I'll not be able. I would not like Stella to think we had forgotten her." She pushed a piece of meat idly through the gravy on her plate, raised it, and laid it back listlessly. She would not meet John's eyes.

He said: "You are thinking of something else. There is some other reason. . . ."

Faith raised her glance. Suddenly there was fear in them, stark and frantic terror, hidden almost instantly behind her forced but gentle smile. She whispered: "Go see her tomorrow. Please, John. For me?"

His hand went out compassionately, brown and strong, to close over her frail and blue-veined one lying so listlessly beside her tray. The terror in Faith's eyes had its revelation for John Cross. Faith now knew the end was near. He fathomed suddenly the reason behind her request that he call on Stella Norden. Stella had been Faith's closest friend and the one who, as the end drew near, Faith hoped might be the woman with whom John might resume the life that had been interrupted by her own long illness.

Divining this, John Cross felt a burning in his eyes and throat. He said hoarsely: "Sure I'll see her, Faith. I'll do it tomorrow."

He took the tray from the bed and carried it to the dresser. He returned to place a gentle kiss on Faith's dry forehead, feeling as he did the burning fever that was in her. Her eyelids drooped. Still smiling, she dropped into a deep sleep even as John Cross watched.

Slowly shaking his head, he blew out the lamp, picked up the tray, and returned downstairs, yet the tightness returned to his throat every time his thoughts returned to Faith and her piteous request. He was a big man who tackled his problems in a direct and roughshod way. But now he was faced with a problem that required a different method of approach, and John Cross was not sure he could manage it.

VI

"Caught Red-Handed"

This morning, Sunday, again there was evidence of carousing in the Norden house. Burt arose at five, passed with an involuntary shudder through the parlor that reeked of spilled whisky, and went out into the crisp and dewy dawn. As soon as the chores were done, he hitched the team to the hired buckboard and climbed up onto the seat for the drive to town. His saddle horse trailed behind, tied to the rear of the buckboard by his reins.

This morning the full weight of pain was in his thigh and had spread upward and downward until it encompassed nearly his entire side and leg. The stitches pulled with little stabs of pain whenever he moved, adding their small irritation to the larger ache of the wound. The bandage turned freshly red from his morning's exertion, and despite the sharp air he grew warm and began to sweat.

At seven, he delivered the team and buckboard to Jed Priest, who eyed his limping friend and said dryly: "Kid, don't head into a killin' fight with nothing but your fists. You ain't going to put out a burning barn with a bucketful of water."

Contrarily the words, so opposite in meaning to those once spoken by his father, had the effect of reminding him of his father's words. "Guns were made for killing . . . mostly for killing men. To carry one advertises the fact that you are prepared to kill." And: "Mostly having no gun will keep you out of trouble."

Now greater even than his fear of Mitch and of Mitch's vengeance was Burt's fear that, if he packed a gun, temper or helplessness or pure hate would make him use it. Then there would be further disgrace for the name of Norden, disgrace unmerited by a father who had carried the name so proudly.

Shrugging impatiently, Burt swung to the gray's back, his leg throbbing painfully, and cantered from the town. Sight of Mrs. Gundersen on the store's narrow porch reminded him of the strays, of his promise to hunt them. He owed the Gundersens nothing, save for a little money as did all the folks in this country, money that would be paid at the end of the season when the cattle had been sold. Yet even this set up its obligations. His thoughts puzzled at this sense of obligation for a while and finally came to the realization that all of a man's relations with others have a way of setting up obligations, however trivial. No one lives entirely alone, for every man, no matter how lonely a life he leads, is dependent to some degree upon the efforts and toiling of others, and for this dependence finds that he owes them something, something that mere money can never repay.

Burt's expression lightened as he mentally explored the ramifications of this newly discovered line of thinking. Miles dropped behind him, and before ten he rode again into the Norden meadow, traversed by its clear and bubbling stream, green with new growth of grass, rising from the stubble of recently cut hay.

Stella would not look at him, but she had the house spotless, and, when he came in, she cut a piece of still-hot apple pie for him and poured him a glass of milk. He ate the pie and drank the milk slowly, thinking all the while of the things he would like to say, thinking he would like to ask her to tell Sam Shirer to stay the hell away.

At the last he was fully aware that he could never reproach

his mother, nor could he make any open attempt at taking the reins of her life from her own hands. Whatever he did, it could never be through her that he did it. If Sam Shirer were to be kept away, then it would have to be a thing between Sam Shirer and Burt himself. *I'll tell him,* he thought hopelessly. *But it won't do any good.*

John Cross came riding into the meadow, and hailed the house from a hundred yards away.

Stella was suddenly younger, suddenly flustered. "Talk to him," she said in a light, soft voice. "I can't have him see me this way. I'll change."

Pride was left in Stella. In happier days there had been close friendship, much travel back and forth between Nordens' N Bar and Clevis Cross. With Faith's sickness and Nick's death this closeness had passed. But the sight of John Cross could bring back its poignant pleasantness to Stella, could make her remember her pride in good, fine things, and make her want to preserve it untarnished by change. Hope stirred in Burt as he went outside to talk to big John Cross.

It occurred to Burt that John Cross's eyes saw too much, but his words gave nothing away. "Your mother here, son? Faith has been wanting to call for some time, but she's ailing and asked me. . . ." His words trailed off as he noted Burt's limp. He said: "Lucy told me to give you her thanks for bringing her safely home last night."

Burt felt himself flushing. He said: "Ma's getting dressed." It seemed to him that this sounded as though Stella were just getting up, and he felt a need to explain further. "She's been cleaning, and wearing an old dress. She didn't want you to see. . . ." He felt himself deeper into the quicksand of confusion.

There seemed to be equal confusion in big John Cross as Stella came to the door, wearing the bright-flowered, full-skirted dress that Burt loved so well and that had been so long put away. His hat came off his head, leaving behind the mark of its pressure on his damp-packed hair. Even Burt could see how hard John Cross tried at picking up threads of unruffled friendship, could see, also, how John Cross failed.

Stella murmured: "Come in, John. How is Faith? I have been meaning to call."

John Cross went through the doorway as Stella stepped aside. Burt hesitated for a moment, hearing the low murmur of their voices in the parlor, then, shrugging, he mounted the gray and took the winding road out of the meadow and up toward the headwaters of the Bear. A mile from the house, where the land dipped, he left the road, taking a narrow trail through the woods.

Here timber grew so thick and so heavy that the ground rarely felt the heat of the sun. There was no grass, no underbrush save for the struggling, small spruces seeded from the larger ones. In spring and early summer, snow lay hard-packed and deep here, long after grass had sprouted in other areas.

This was an area of perpetual half darkness, the deep and brooding shadow of primeval forest. This was an area untouched since the beginning of time, where the giant spruces seeded and grew, matured and died, and rotted where they fell. Impenetrable, heavy with the smell of resin, of rotted mulch underfoot two feet thick, the place had an unpleasant, depressing effect upon Burt.

He hurried because of it, and in this way covered the distance from bottom to top, something over five miles, in less than an hour. He came out upon the chill bareness of Timberline Ridge in late morning, and paused to rest his horse.

Now, with an excellent view of the country for miles, he considered it for a possible outlet. Timberline Ridge, bare and windswept at its top, marched off to the north for a full twenty-five miles before it began to bend to embrace the headwaters of the Bear on the right, the beginnings of Clear Creek on the left. Clear Creek wound southward through first Riorsons' Rocking R, then Clevis Cross. Up there in haze-shrouded distance, it continued this bend to the leftward, like a gigantic horseshoe, to enclose completely the valley of Clear Creek.

On both sides, roughly opposite to the tiny, distance-dwarfed buildings of Clevis Cross, Timberline Ridge began to fall sharply, until on the same side it embraced into its timbered anonymity the road between N Bar and Clevis Cross, and on the other, farther side, the pass, which led with sinuous, twisting indirectness to the silver camps on the far slopes of the Continental Divide.

All of the trails, numbering less than half a dozen in all, and the two roads, were effectively fenced by timber and by the timber's impenetrable wall of deadfalls. An impossible thing, thought Burt, for a man to drive cattle from this valley ahead without leaving the plain tracks of his passing. Yet it was being done, every day and every week.

As was the case in the valley of the Bear where the Nordens' outfit lay and the town of Mustang, this valley of Clear Creek was also marred and pitted with mine dumps and the pockmarks of prospect holes. A road led from its upper reaches, winding downcountry across the vast, grassy bottom like a tiny, gray-brown thread. The creek followed effortlessly the lowest ground, spreading here and there into beaver ponds that glistened blue and silver in the late morning sunlight.

Burt nudged his horse, and the animal moved across the mile-wide bare and rolling ridge top, and dropped into thinning, clearing-dotted timber for the descent. A band of elk raised their massive heads to stare as Burt passed, then moved with unhurried and stately grace into the protective screen of spruce.

Burt had searched the country ceaselessly and thoroughly all this time with his narrowed eyes, and was therefore surprised when he saw the two riders on the far side of the valley. He immediately thought of Mitch Riorson, and of Jed Priest's cautious admonition: *Don't ever let 'em rig you into a fight where there ain't other people around to see you get a fair shake.*

Recalling this, he immediately reined his horse into the trees, descending through them, mentally marking the place where he had last seen Mitch and his brother. He glimpsed them twice, leisurely riding downcountry and, at last having satisfied himself that they were far enough away to make discovery of himself extremely unlikely, he broke into the open and trotted his horse across the valley floor.

All of the cattle in this valley watered in Clear Creek, and, as he crossed it, he encountered a bunch of perhaps thirty, nooning in the shade of the willows. It is a cattleman's instinctive habit to read the brands on everything he sees. Burt did this, circling through the bunch, and finally satisfied that there was none of his went on toward the stand of timber.

Just inside the timber fringe on the far side of the valley, he cut Mitch's fresh trail, and curiously turned along it upcountry. His intent today was riding, and one direction, one trail was as good as any other.

This trail rose gradually, and, when Mitch's horse's tracks left the trail, Burt left it, too. After a stiff climb of nearly a mile, he reached the foot of a gray and rocky mine dump, completely losing the prints he had been following in the rocks and gravel. He stopped, shrugged, and was about to turn back when he heard the branch snap behind him.

He whirled, startled. Below him, not fifty feet away, Mitch

Riorson sat his horse. Cradled loosely in his arms, Mitch held a rifle. His face was a study of hate and rage and something new that was puzzling to Burt—fear. Behind Mitch sat younger Chuck Riorson, also holding a rifle. Wordless, Mitch raised the gun. Chuck edged his horse ten feet to one side, and followed suit. Two rifles were trained on Burt.

Words crowded to Burt's lips. "Wait! You're not going to. . . ."

It came to him with terrifying clarity that Mitch intended to kill him. It was the one impression that registered in his startled brain. Then his horse leaped and shied at the savagery of frantic spurs. A shot made its harsh racket, another, and Burt was into the trees, lying low against his horse's neck, entirely unconscious of the clawing branches that tore at him and sought to unseat him and fling him into the trail. Behind came the sound of pursuit, and Mitch's raging and vicious words: "Don't let him get away!"

VII

"Boxed"

Odd was the feeling in John Cross, the feeling that the country had done Stella Norden an injustice as he rode back toward Clevis Creek that afternoon. In John Cross was nothing of narrow-mindedness, yet in him as in all men of this country there were strong feelings as to what a woman's conduct should be. Stella violated those standards, yet Cross, after this afternoon, could not find it in his heart to condemn her. Instead, she had charmed him with her gentle womanliness; she had made him see the side of her the country had forgotten or had not known existed.

In late afternoon he came into the yard at Clevis Cross, and Lucy ran out to meet him, her eyes bright with tears, her face set in a mold of concern. "You had better look at Mother, Dad. I sent Dorian for the doctor. She's weaker. Her voice is only a whisper now." The girl buried her face in his rough shirt. "Dad, I'm scared."

His comforting of Lucy was brief, and then he raced up the stairs to Faith's room with Lucy close behind him. At her door he stopped, composing himself, but filled with the same terror of loss that Lucy was experiencing. When he went in, he saw immediately that his daughter had not exaggerated her mother's condition. Faith lay, thin and motionless, beneath the single sheet, her skin white and transparent, her eyes closed. At his entry, she opened her eyes and smiled faintly. Her voice was a barely audible murmur. "John, take my hand."

He knelt beside the bed, taking her two emaciated hands within his own strong brown ones. "The doctor's coming. You will be all right."

The shake of her head was hardly noticeable. "Not this time, John. Not this time. There is nothing a doctor can do for me now."

He moved as if to rise. "I'll get you some broth." But sudden strength came to her hands as she held him there. Fright was in her voice, fright that was a child's fear of the unknown.

"We should not have to make this journey alone, John."

"You are making no journey." Emotion was hoarseness in his voice, dryness of his throat, a stinging behind his eyes. He could see now, looking for it, how Faith had weakened and slipped in these last thirty days. Seeing her every day, the change had been so gradual that it now came to him with a shock as he comprehended the full extent of her failing and the inevitable result.

"John, let's not fool ourselves." She smiled to take the sting from this, squeezed his hand to silence his protest. Her voice grew even weaker as she said: "Stella Norden is lonely. You will be lonely, and Lucy will need a good woman's care. Will you be nice to Stella, John? Will you promise me you'll try?"

At this moment, thought of another woman was abomination to John Cross. The empty, soothing agreement with Faith's whim came automatically to his lips, but he stopped it there, seeing at last the terrible urgency that was in her eyes, the pleading. *Why, she wants this more than anything else in the world* was his thought.

The thought silenced him, and the moments dragged. Weak was the pressure of Faith's grasp, ever weaker. Yet her will forced the demand: "Promise, John?"

"If that is what you want, then I will promise. Perhaps Stella will not have me, but I will do my best. But not right away, Faith. Not right away."

"All right, John." A light smile lifted the corners of her mouth, the mouth that was still sweet. Her breathing slowed and stopped, and her heart was still. Suddenly John Cross, big John Cross buried his face against her breast and wept, the sound of it terrible and lost in the utter quiet of the house at Clevis Cross.

Burt Norden had abandoned his horse, had with his quirt sent it crashing downhill through the timber while he himself paralleled the slope on soundless feet. This action gave him ten minutes, but it also deprived him of his mobility.

Now swiftly running downcountry through the timber, soft-footed on the rotted mulch of pine needles, he knew the panic, the sheer terror of a hunted animal. Below the mine dump where Mitch had caught him, he cut a trail, pounded plain by the hoofs of cattle and horses, and paused here momentarily to still his gusty breathing.

Below him he could hear the thrashing of Mitch and Chuck Riorson, and then the enraged bellow of Mitch as he found Burt's riderless horse. They would be returning now, returning to seek him out.

Puzzlement stirred in Burt as he crouched in a heavy tangle of downed timber. Why was Mitch so suddenly determined to kill? It stretched even Burt's imagination to believe this was the outcome of last night's fight. Yet what did he know of the things defeat and humiliation could breed in a mind as twisted and vicious as Mitch Riorson's?

Horseback, they could not pursue him into this jungle of deadfalls. He waited until their crashing passage had faded with distance, then rose and made his precarious, inching way a quarter of a mile farther. He could hear them above him, paralleling his own course. Abruptly he came upon a clearing, long and narrow, that reached its scar-like bareness clear to the Timberline Ridge, far above.

Halted at its edge, fearing to emerge into the open, he heard Mitch's voice as a hoarse whisper from higher on the slope. "He's got to cross that clearing, or he's got to go back. Take your horse and swing back. A mile or so beyond the mine the timber thins out, and it's nothing but scrub brush for a quarter mile. Find yourself a spot and watch that brush so he don't try to get away upcountry. I'll sit here with the rifle and wait until he comes out."

Burt frowned. With Mitch watching this clearing, Chuck the brush farther north, they had him neatly boxed on two sides, which left him two poorer alternatives. Uphill at least for a mile, having to pass Mitch on the way, or downhill, where he would be exposed entirely while he crossed the grassy valley floor. Afoot, he would be slow and clumsy, easily overtaken by the Riorsons with their horses.

Chuck had led Burt's own horse away and, Burt thought, would undoubtedly tie him somewhere near to the place where he took up his vigil, in plain sight, for Chuck was no more of a fool than Mitch. Recovering his own horse was, then, out of the question.

Driving through his trapped feeling, his growing fear, came a strange recognition of this particular place. Straight downhill across this bare slash of clearing, and almost to the bottom, stood a huge, round boulder, a full ten feet high. For a couple of minutes Burt stared at the boulder, preoccupied with his own trouble, with this preoccupation slowing recognition in him. When it came, it came with a rush. Down there, on the downhill side of that boulder, he had found his father's body, riddled and stiff and crusted with dried blood. The boulder looked oddly different from above, and perhaps this had slowed the remembrance in Burt.

A connection troubled him, the apparent coincidence of being beset himself at the same approximate spot in which his father had met death. *I wonder if the Riorsons killed him?* was his instant thought, which he rejected as the succeeding question occurred. *But why? He never had any trouble with them.*

Eventually the urgency of his own trouble drove thought of his father from his mind, and he gave consideration to extricating himself from the jaws of this loose-spring trap. Downhill, and across the valley, was out of the question, he decided. A run across the scar of clearing was equally impossible. Which left him but one alternative—uphill, straight past the watchful and armed figure of Mitch.

His decision made for him by circumstances, he no longer troubled himself with doubt. Stooping, he slipped off his boots. With his knife he cut a thong of leather from his belt and with it strung the boots around his neck. Then, taking infinite care with the placing of his feet in the dead tangle of timber and brush, he commenced the slow and tortuous climb.

Half an hour passed—an hour. Burt calculated he had gone less than a quarter mile, but he could congratulate himself, for he had made no noise, however small. His breathing was shallow and fast, but quiet. Tenseness rode him. He would go ten or fifteen steps, then stop to watch and to listen. It was during one of these stops that he heard Mitch Riorson's restless stirring not two hundred yards away. The light and pleasant aroma of tobacco smoke drifted to him. After another five careful paces he came upon a trail, twisting and open, and down it glimpsed a flash of Mitch Riorson's blue shirt.

He froze. Movement stirred the shirt, and Burt thought: *If*

I only had me a rifle! But caution told him: *Wait.* This he ignored, driven by the rising impatience, the growing anger that was in him. He started up, only to settle back, appalled at the rashness that had almost controlled him. *I wouldn't get closer than fifty yards to him. Then he'd get me.*

He turned and squatted carefully, taking a position that would not tire him or cramp his legs. A deer fly buzzed idly and settled on his bare hand. Burt carefully brushed it away. Along the trail Mitch Riorson cursed softly and steadily.

Chuck's voice brought its worried cadences along the trail from the distant, brushy slide. "You see him at all, Mitch? You heard him?"

Mitch called: "Naw! But stay put! He can't get away."

The sun floated hotly downward toward the high-ridged bowl, and at last tipped its flaming edge below it. With its movement now visible it sank steadily from sight. Immediately the rare air turned cool, and shadow settled itself in the timber.

Chuck Riorson's voice came again. "Mitch, he'll get away in the dark. What do we do now?"

"Hell, he's afoot, ain't he? Quit worrying. We'll pick him up."

Burt waited and, as the light faded from the sky, heard Chuck come along the trail, pulling Burt's own gray behind. They passed him a scant ten feet away. As the gray went by, Burt came noiselessly to his feet and stepped into the trail. Running, he caught at the gray's reins with an out-flung hand, yanking viciously the instant his grasp felt leather. The gray had reared, adding his own strength to the pull against the rein ends in Chuck's hand.

They came free, and with ease and speed born of long familiarity Burt separated them and swung to the gray's back, at the same time turning him in a tight circle. Chuck's voice told him that Chuck still remained unaware of what was happening, for Chuck cursed the gray in a voice that held no alarm, only an ill-tempered uneasiness.

A bend in the trail, and the half light of dusk combined to aid Burt unexpectedly, as did his crouching position on the gray's back and the dark clothes he wore. Chuck howled: "Somethin' spooked that damned gray! He's got away from me!"

"Well, get him! Get him! If you don't, Burt Norden will!"

VIII

"Escape"

Burt, crouching against the gray's neck, pounded along the trail at a run. Behind him, growing faint as distance increased, he could hear the hoofs of Chuck's horse, and farther still Mitch Riorson's ragged shouting.

He came to a fork in the trail, seeing this dimly, and unhesitatingly took the lower fork. He had no appetite for further skulking in the timber high on the ridge, wanting only to reach the unhampering freedom of open grass, where he could run downcountry along the road for the sanctuary of Clevis Cross.

He came to another fork in the trail just above the bare outline of the mine dump where Mitch and Chuck had surprised him, and again he took the lower trail, here making his mistake. For the lower trail led only into the mine workings, the upper circling above and then plunging onto the plain.

The gray galloped along the trail, for two hundred yards, then bringing itself up short, sliding in the rubble, before a towering frame structure. Below this the mine stretched away for a full quarter mile downhill, crested with the tracks of the narrow-gauge mine railway. A couple of rusty mine cars made their sagging dim shapes against the lighter color of the rock dump.

Burt breathed—"Damn it."—sawing the gray's head around and pointing him back uptrail. He had gone but a scant fifty yards when he heard the pound of Chuck's horse as the younger of the two Riorsons came thundering along. He heard Chuck stop at the fork, saw the flare of a match as Chuck dismounted to search the trail for the gray's tracks.

He still doesn't know I've got the horse he thought, but turned back, knowing that Chuck would find the gray's tracks and would take this lower trail. He was neatly boxed, and knew it. A stand beside the trail, hand covering his horse's nostrils, might keep Chuck's notice from him until Chuck had passed. But to bolt back up the trail would put him directly into Mitch's path, for Mitch could be no more than a hundred yards behind Chuck.

Desperation touched him; panic ran its brief course through him. Yet it was not his nature to give up. With the gray again pointed at the mine, he searched the ground for tracks, for the sign of a continuation of this trail. There was too much dark for tracks, yet he did see the pale path that swung around the mine building, and took it, well aware that he could never be worse off than he now was.

The horse grew spooky as the trail dipped sharply across the edge of the dump, and placed his hoofs cautiously in the loose rubble. Then suddenly Burt could see ahead of him a trail that was dark with horse and cattle droppings, plain and smooth from much usage. Puzzled, he halted. This trail but touched the one he was on briefly before it continued its own upward way. Staring, straining his eyes in the near darkness, Burt followed its devious path with his glance. In wide and easy-graded loops it coursed upward, to end apparently in the black, yawning mouth of the mine tunnel.

He shrugged, much relieved, and reined his horse downward toward this path, spurring instantly as the horse came into it and feeling the lift in his spirits as the distance flowed swiftly behind. Relief was solid and tangible in Burt, something that took strength from him, made him feel his overpowering weariness, the renewed pain of the wound in his thigh. Yet in the back of his consciousness a vague knowledge persisted, a fleeting, unrecognized awareness that would not take shape. He had gazed upon the outlet from this valley, upon the rustler's run and did not know that he had. He had seen the thing his father had seen, and, because he had, his life was forfeit. He had seen the rustler's run, and sometime he would know what he had seen. But not tonight. For the terror of being hunted game was still with him, and his only thought was to get away.

Dorian brought Doc Brady to Clevis Cross, and then, at John Cross's quiet suggestion, went to fetch Stella Norden.

Lucy crouched in a big, leather-covered chair in the corner, head down upon her arms, sobbing softly and without cessation. John Cross stared into the leaping fire, his eyes bitter and blank. Doc Brady stood with his back to the fire, rubbing the hands that were clasped together behind him against each other, in a gesture that was purely automatic. He said: "John, at a time like this I hate being a doctor. I don't know enough to be a doctor. No man does. If we did, I might have saved her. Someday doctors will be able to save cases like hers."

John Cross murmured wearily: "Doc, it isn't your fault. Stop blaming yourself." He scowled. "I was thinking of Stella Norden. If she felt like I feel, then I can understand a lot of things I never understood before. There is something gone out of me. It is as though my heart were cut out, and nothing left in its place. Maybe it would be easy to believe that whisky could fill that hollow."

Doc murmured: "I never blamed Stella. But you can't let Faith down like that, John. Life goes on. It's got to go on. You are not the first who has lost a loved one. You will not be the last. You can never replace Faith, but you've got to try as much for her sake and Lucy's as your own."

Cross shook his head, never lifting his eyes from the fire, and Doc did not protest. This was not the time. There is a time for grieving and a time to stop grieving, as Doc well knew. He said: "You don't need me here. I'll come back tomorrow and help you bring her to town."

He picked up his hat from the table, touched John Cross's shoulder as he went by. He stopped before the forlorn figure of Lucy for a moment, looking down. Then, shrugging at his helplessness, he walked across the room to the door.

His buggy horse was tied to the porch rail by a short length of rope. He untied this and climbed to a seat, taking up the reins. As he went up the steep road into the timber, he passed Dorian's buckboard and could see the woman's shape of Stella Norden beside the foreman. Doc Brady smiled a little as he acknowledged Dorian's shout and upraised hand. Nothing like someone else's troubles to take your mind from your own. Stella would discover this in the days to come.

Upon entering the house, Stella's eyes went immediately to John Cross, bitter-eyed and brooding before the fire. Compassion instantly softened her expression, saddened her eyes.

A soft sobbing on the far side of the room claimed her attention, and, seeing Lucy, there was no hesitation in her. Immediately she crossed the room and sank to her knees on the floor before the girl. Like a child, Lucy came forward against her, burying her tear-stained face against Stella's welcome feminine softness. For a long moment, Stella comforted her, finally rising to her feet and pulling Lucy up with her.

She spoke in a brisk near-whisper. "There. Come into the kitchen with me while I fix you and your father something to eat."

Cross turned his head, saying: "Nothing for me, Stell."

"Hush! You'll eat if I have to feed you myself."

Her words drew a faint smile from Lucy, a smile that was vastly encouraging to Stella. The girl said: "You needn't have gone to all the trouble of. . . ."

"Trouble? Why, girl, this is no trouble. You need me, don't you?"

Perhaps, she thought, this was the thing that had been lacking in her own life. Perhaps she was a woman who required the need of others, something beyond the casual and understanding need of an eighteen-year-old boy.

The smell of coffee filled the kitchen, wafting through into the big front room. It brought John Cross out into the kitchen, stifling his grief for the sake of manners. And in a little while they made a compact and friendly group, drawn closer tonight by the trouble that had come, unbidden, to point up their need for one another.

At nine, Burt came pounding into the yard at Clevis Cross with the heavy weariness of this long afternoon of terror upon him. Dorian intercepted him, gave him a hand down from his saddle, and took the reins of his horse.

Burt said hoarsely: "They're after me! Mitch and Chuck Riorson . . . with rifles. They tried to kill me."

"Why, son, I doubt that. They're mean, but they're not fools. Mebbe they just wanted you to think they were tryin' to kill you."

Helpless impatience stirred in Burt. "They tried. I tell you . . . they shot at me."

"Why? Why would they want to kill you? Because of that fight at the dance last night?" Dorian shook his head in the darkness, a gesture felt rather than seen.

Burt's shoulders slumped. His own conviction had not

lessened, but he could see the futility of trying to convince this man, of trying to convince John Cross. Within his own mind had been amazement as he had realized Mitch meant to kill him, for he had not yet fathomed the reason. He said wearily: "Give me the reins. I've got to get home."

"No need of that. Missus Cross died tonight. Your mother's here."

Shock and surprise—and youth's awe in the face of death—held Burt silent for a moment. Then he said: "The chores. The cow's got to be milked, the rest of the stuff fed. . . ."

"I did that for you when I went after your ma. I'll put your horse away." He moved off into the darkness toward the corral, leading Burt's lathered and weary gray. Burt watched his shape lose identity in the shroud of night, then turned reluctantly toward the house.

He would not mention either Mitch or Chuck. He had made a fool of himself in Dorian's eyes. A scared kid—that was what Dorian thought him. He would not have Lucy thinking that—or John Cross, either. For tonight he was safe. Tomorrow . . . ?

He went into the kitchen, into the warm and fragrant room where only yesterday he had quarreled with Lucy. He felt clumsy and awkward. He looked at John Cross, then shifted his glance to his mother, still avoiding Lucy's eyes. Stella Norden said: "Where have you been? You look awful. What's the matter with your leg?"

"Hurt it. I been riding." He pulled his glance around, forced it to rest upon Lucy. Her paleness shocked him, stirred his love, awoke his compassion. He said clumsily: "Lucy, I'm sorry."

Tears brightened her eyes. Stella forestalled her new outburst by saying: "There. Enough of that. It is time you were in bed, Lucy. Tomorrow is another day."

She led Lucy from the kitchen, and Burt could hear them climbing the stairs. John Cross said—"You can sleep in the ranch office, son."—and led the way, opening the door onto the tiny cubbyhole where papers and spurs, chaps and old hats and boots made their comfortably untidy litter. Burt removed his boots and, when John Cross had closed the door behind him, lay down fully dressed upon the leather-covered settee.

The riddle of Mitch's ill-concealed murderous intent puzzled him as did this disturbing conviction that he held the answer in his head—if only he could find it. Still puzzled, still troubled, at last he fell asleep. . . .

IX

"Tunnel Target"

At four, the eastern sky was a gray line, bringing into ghostly silhouette the tall, ragged line of spruces on the ridge top. The hillsides still clung to their mantle of darkness, but down in the valley, and in the yard at Clevis Cross, objects began to take shape, dimly at first, but with rapidly increasing clarity. This faint light woke Burt at once. Unmoving, he lay still for a moment, staring about him at the dim and unrecognized clutter of John Cross's office.

It had been a night of flight for Burt. Dreams and nightmares had thrice awakened him, bathed with sweat and shaking from head to foot. Now, suddenly, he knew where he was, knew that Faith Cross was dead, and that Mitch and Chuck Riorson were determined to kill him.

Still dazed from sudden awakening, his mind was mostly relaxed, and in this relaxed state came suddenly upon the thing that had so effectively eluded him last night. The trail. The trail he had taken from the mine—the one that led upward to disappear into the mine tunnel. It was still a puzzle, for how could men rustle cattle by driving them into a mine tunnel? Yet he could not rid himself of the conviction that somewhere in that old abandoned mine tunnel laid the answer to the rustling that had plagued the country so long. Also, it was there that the answer to Mitch's and Chuck's attempt to murder him the night before would be found. There might be the solution to Nick Norden's murder, for it was not a quarter mile from the tunnel mouth to the huge boulder that had sheltered Nick's dead body, more than a year ago.

Convulsively Burt came to his feet. No sound broke the silence of this house as he walked through the big front room to the door, carrying his boots. Beside the door stood John Cross's carbine, and on the table beside it was a handful of shells. Burt hesitated, then snatched up the rifle, and stuffed the shells into his pocket.

The air outside was chill, and Burt's breath preceded him in great, steamy clouds. He could hear a stir of early movement from the bunkhouse, and ran lightly across the yard to the corral. His saddle lay on the top rail beside the gate, his bridle hanging from the horn, and the saddle blanket was across the top to protect the saddle and bridle from rain and dew.

His gray was alone in this corral, and easily caught. Mounted, he went out of the yard, taking the road up the valley, just as Dorian opened the bunkhouse door. He did not know whether Dorian saw him or not, and did not care. He let the gray, freshened by a night's rest and a good feed of hay and grain, stretch out, but as he approached the Riorsons' place, he left the road and made a big circle to the right, wasting a full hour of time, but succeeding in staying entirely out of sight of the house.

The sun came up and warmed his back. The heavy, high-country dew disappeared from the grass, and the timber sent its sharp, resin smell flowing down the slopes, pungently strong and pleasant. Cattle, fat and sleek, roamed the valley in early morning coolness, grazing. As the day's heat increased, they would seek the shade and coolness of the timber.

It was hard for Burt to believe, amid this peaceful beauty, that along this same road he had galloped only last night with death at his heels. Thinking thus, his head swiveled around, now nervously watching the road behind, and all of the goodness of the morning was gone, only fear remained. Strong was his desire to turn his horse, to sink his spurs, to return to the safety of Clevis Cross. Only stubbornness forced him on and awareness that Mitch would hunt him down, somewhere, sometime. His only salvation lay in discovery of the mine tunnel's secret, so that he could go to John Cross, to old man Guiry, to the others for help. Yet he could not control the nervous and constant turning of his head, the side-to-side shifting of his eyes. He could not control the fear that made him start at each small noise.

At eight, he came to the trail that led upward to the mine, the trail that showed so much plain evidence of travel. A few moments later he found the reason why it had never been followed and explored. A quarter mile below the mine it forked, the right fork continuing on upcountry, well-traveled and plain, the left, for as far as the eye could see, having been carefully worked upon to erase the plain signs of usage. A casual rider would notice none of this. Only because Burt remembered the way he had come down last night was he able to detect it.

He turned his horse and after a hundred yards came to the place where the trail again showed its heavy usage. Feeling excitement, he gigged the horse sharply onward, and shortly came to the yawning mouth of the tunnel.

He hesitated. At that moment he heard a shout behind him, faint across the distance, and the bawl of a cow. Screened by timber, he could see nothing beyond it. But with his hesitation suddenly gone, he reined and spurred his reluctant horse into the suddenly complete darkness and rode along the gently sloping timbered tunnel.

A slight bend blotted out the square of light that was the

tunnel mouth, and complete darkness settled upon Burt. Somewhere he could hear water running, splashing against the rocks. There was a damp and dank smell here, but there was another odor as well, the corral smell of manure, the smell of horses and cattle.

The path underfoot was beaten and churned by the many hoofs that had preceded Burt through here. Perhaps it was this that took the fear and hesitation from the gray, for the animal, his first skittishness abated, went along at a steady, plodding walk, for all the world as though he were patiently plodding down the long road toward Mustang.

Seconds were hours, minutes eternities. After what he judged to be fifteen minutes, Burt heard an odd rumble behind him, a deep murmur of sound. Turned nervous and afraid, he kicked the gray's ribs, and the animal broke into a trot. Suddenly the air seemed fresher, warmer, and with no warning whatever Burt came around a sharp turn and saw ahead of him a square of bright sunlight.

Here he came upon a fork in the tunnel, the right fork continuing blackly into the bowels of the mountain, the left fork, freshly timbered, plainly a recent excavation, taking its two-hundred-yard straight way to the opening. The story was plain now. Somehow old man Riorson, by calculations and explorations, had discovered how close this tunnel came to going straight through the mountain. He and his three boys had finished it out, perhaps no longer ago than two or three years, timbered it, and begun running cattle through it.

By pure accident, while hunting strays, Nick Norden had come upon it, had been discovered, and murdered for the knowledge he possessed. As simple as this, then, was the enigma of vanishing cattle. Once through the mountain, beyond the bare, telltale summit of Timberline Ridge, the cattle were driven to the road that sinuously led to the silver camps on the Continental Divide. At Silver City there was a steady and continuing market for beef. The Riorsons had been able to control their greed. They had taken only small bunches and, because they had, were able to escape detection completely.

The murmur of sounds increased behind Burt, and abruptly he knew it for what it was, the combined bellow of cattle and the shouting of drovers. He came out of the tunnel into bright sunlight, blinking his eyes against the glare.

Regaining his sight, he stared upward toward the summit of Timberline Ridge, towering three thousand feet above him. He half reined his horse around, intending for a moment to ride up over it, but then realization struck him that the journey which had taken him a mere fifteen minutes through the tunnel would take him a full three hours over the top. *If I go that way,* he thought, *by the time I can get back to Clevis Cross, they'll all be gone to Mustang for the funeral.* Burt could realize that proof was important. If he could return to Clevis Cross and bring John Cross here in time to track the Riorsons and catch them with the stolen herd, then there would be no wiggling out of it for them.

With his mind suddenly made up, he swung the gray and pointed him straight back into the tunnel, spurring and forcing the animal to a fast trot in the darkness. With his eyes blinded, he nearly missed the fork, going past it and only apprised of its presence by the draft of cold air issuing from the old tunnel.

Before him, the steady plod of cattle hoofs, the harrying shouts of the Riorsons, were loud and near. Suddenly frightened and regretful, but with his decision unshaken, Burt reined his horse into the old tunnel and stopped, far enough back to be invisible in the darkness, close enough to see and identify the Riorsons as they went past.

The thunder of plodding and softly lowing cattle increased, reverberating and echoing and multiplying in this confined space. Visible in the faint light from the open tunnel mouth, the leaders went past. Burt counted one, two, three, four, and reached a count of sixteen by the time the first rider went past. This rider was Chuck Riorson, and immediately behind him was Mitch. Old Dan Riorson brought up the rear. Sim, the youngest, had either been left at the ranch, or on guard at the far mouth of the tunnel.

Burt was forced to admire the Riorsons' sagacity. Today they knew there would be no riders, no snoopers in the Clear Creek Valley. Faith Cross was dead, today the day of the funeral.

Dan Riorson's broad back was presented to Burt, diminishing against the light at the tunnel mouth. Burt started a sigh of relief, and then, suddenly, horror halted it, horror and a trapped and terrible fear. Something must have brought to Burt's gray the scent of other horses, for at this instant he raised his head and nickered. Before Burt could reach him in the dark, before he could stifle and stop the gray's nostrils with his hand, the horse nickered again.

He caught the animal then, but it was too late. Dan Riorson swung in his saddle, and over the murmur of the cattle came his surprised: "Hey! What the hell? I told Sim to stay at the tunnel mouth." He gave his orders swiftly and sharply. "Chuck, take 'em on out. Push 'em easy so we can catch up. Mitch, ride back through and see if Sim's still there. Watch yourself. If it ain't Sim . . ."—he broke off—"hell, it couldn't be anyone else. Sim would've used his gun before he let anyone into the tunnel. Well, go on! We ain't got all day."

Burt saw Mitch go past the fork in the tunnel and disappear into the darkness of the main shaft. His trapped feeling increased. He fingered the carbine, and absently shoved shells into its magazine. The end to this was plain and sure. When Mitch returned, old Dan would realize that the nicker could have come from but one place—the old tunnel. Then Burt would be trapped.

Decision steadied his nerves. He raised the carbine, but found that in this darkness he could not get his sights. Dan's body made an utterly black blob against the dimly reflected light from the tunnel mouth. He, therefore, sighted against the lightness just beside Dan, and then shifted the rifle ever so slightly before he pulled the trigger.

The flash and the roar of the carbine seemed to fill this narrow tunnel. The acrid smoke made a cloud that hid Dan from him entirely for a full half minute. When it cleared, Dan was gone.

Burt swung to the gray's back and started out. *I've got a chance now* was his thought. *Chuck's at one end, Mitch the other. All I've got to do is take care of Mitch.*

But as he came into the light at the tunnel fork, something splatted against the rock wall at his side, showering him with sharp rock splinters. Suddenly he realized with a complete cessation of hope: *I missed him. I missed Dan, and now I'm done for.*

X

"Rustlers' Showdown"

Doc Brady came out at nine, a casket in the back of the buckboard he drove, with Solly Juhan, the undertaker, in the seat beside him. Doc and Dorian carried the casket into the house, and after a while Doc, Dorian, John Cross, and Juhan carried it back out and placed it in the buckboard.

Doc took up the reins, speaking down at John Cross: "I guess two o'clock will be all right, John. Most folks will be able to get away in the afternoon."

He drove away, his going leaving a vast emptiness in John Cross. This was final. Faith was gone. Stella Norden stood beside him, her comforting hand on his arm. Lucy, clinging to Stella, wept anew.

With some apparent thought of breaking the tension, Stella asked: "Why, I don't believe I've seen Burt this morning. Where is he?"

Cross grunted, his mind only half on the question: "Haven't seen him, either."

Dorian, grizzled and stolid, said: "He rode out at daybreak. Don't guess he saw me. He was packing your carbine, John."

Lucy stopped crying abruptly. Cross felt a touch of uneasiness. Dorian went on: "He come to me with a story of the Riorsons trying to kill him yesterday. I didn't pay much mind, figgered he was imagining things. Still, a carbine. . . ."

Lucy cried: "Dad, Mitch tried to kill him with a knife at the dance!"

Stella's hand tightened on Cross's arm. She asked: "John, did he?"

"He had a knee gash on his leg. Doc sewed it up."

So long was Stella silent that John Cross turned uneasy. Her face was bitter and ashamed. She murmured: "I've not been much of a mother. I've not been much of a mother for a long time. But that is going to change." She looked up suddenly at him, with tears glistening in her eyes. "John, I hate to ask it at a time like this, but do you suppose . . . ?"

"I could go after him?" he finished for her because she hesitated. "Sure." He turned abruptly to Dorian. "Saddle my sorrel. Get three or four of the boys and come along."

He found himself welcoming the diversion, although he could not think Burt was in any danger. He smiled at Stella, trying to show her some reassurance. She was a worried mother who was no longer thinking of herself and of her own grief. And she was still attractive, thought John Cross.

He calculated the time he had, before he was due at Mustang, and put his horse into a lope that he varied at intervals by trotting and walking. Dorian rode directly behind him, and strung out behind Dorian rode three Clevis Cross 'punchers.

He rode openly into Riorsons' yard and hailed the house peremptorily, receiving no answer. Concern mounted within him. He had fully expected to find at least a part of the Riorson family at home, and finding them there would have partially convinced him that Burt was imagining things. Yet to find them all gone. . . .

The puzzle of the rustling recurred in his mind, and with it came his own unvoiced suspicion of the Riorsons. There had never been one concrete thing that would tie them in with it, yet his suspicion of them remained.

At the junction of Riorsons' lane with the main road, his sharp eyes detected on the hard-packed ground the hoofprints of three or four horses, hard-pressed, as they came from the lane and onto the road.

He made his decision with characteristic suddenness, saying over his shoulder to Dorian: "We'll follow these until we find the Riorsons."

Burt knew that three of them at least—Dan, Mitch, and Sim—were out there now. He supposed Chuck was still with the cattle. He could hear them talking in low tones, planning, perhaps, how they would rid themselves of him. He could distinguish a part of Dan's talk, for the father's voice had a peculiar, penetrating timbre and was pitched higher than either of his sons' voices. He caught the words: "Mitch, remember where we cached that dynamite that was left when we finished the tunnel? Go get it. We'll seal that nosy Norden kid in here."

Stark terror made a clammy chill along Burt's spine. Silence lay in the tunnel then, and some ten minutes later he heard Mitch's scuffling approach and the rumble of his voice. Dan Riorson appeared briefly against the dim light at the forks, and automatically Burt brought up the carbine and threw a shot at him. Dan cursed, dropped, and crawled to safety.

Mitch's voice raised: "How the hell we goin' to drill the holes with him shootin' at us?"

Another silence, broken by whispers, and finally Dan's voice, heavy with satisfaction: "Gimme a couple of sticks and a piece of fuse. I'll raise so damned much dust in there he won't be able to see a thing."

Another wait for Burt—an agonizing wait, and again

Dan's voice: "Not that much fuse! You want him to toss it back out at us?"

Burt had planned just this, had inched himself forward in the tunnel to wait. Now he backed away again, until he could feel the nervous warmth of the gray beside him. A spark arched into the tunnel. Burt crouched and covered his ears.

The roar was deafening. It filled the tunnel, solid and terrible, and loosened rocks overhead. It lifted dust in a blinding cloud. Even when it was gone, the sound of it still rang in Burt's ears, partially hiding the rumble of falling rock. The blast's acrid smoke rolled along the tunnel with the dust and, when it reached Burt, sent him into a coughing spasm that doubled him over, made him gasp for breath. The gray stampeded back into the tunnel, its hoof beats slowly diminishing, nickering shrilly.

Blindly Burt brought up the carbine, shot, levered, and shot again. His bullets ricocheted off the rock walls of the tunnel and sang away to end abruptly as they reached the forks.

Mitch yelled: "Hurry! He's shootin' again!"

Suddenly Burt was calm. He knew now that there was no way out of this for him. They were too many, and they held all the cards. He thought of Nick Norden, and of the things his death had done to Stella. Upon the Riorsons was the blame for all of this—the blame for what was now happening to him. Anger began to crowd out the fear in Burt. That anger built and grew until it consumed him.

The dust was a curtain. If it could hide the Riorsons, it could also hide Burt. He moved toward the forks, rifle held across his chest, and, as he moved, his leg began to pain again. Yet this only served to increase his anger.

The dust grew thicker, and he stifled a cough. He heard the steady *clang* of hammer against rock drill, seemingly only a few feet from him. He remembered that the carbine was empty and felt his knees go weak, considering what would have happened had he not thought of this in time. He reloaded, and, as he levered a shell into the chamber cautiously and slowly, the click of the mechanism was plainly audible.

Dan's voice came sharply: "What was that?"

Burt stepped into the clearer air of the forks, saw Dan kneeling, rock drill in one hand, hammer in the other. Mitch was silhouetted in the light from the opening. Sim knelt beside the dynamite box.

Burt said—"Hold it!"—never knowing which way to point the rifle, loosely holding it before him. A curse rumbled from Dan's heavy lips, and his hand came back, the hand that held the hammer. Burt forced his glance from Dan, saw Mitch clawing out his revolver, saw Sim, the youngest, rising, fisting paper-wrapped sticks of dynamite in both hands.

He barked—"Hold it!"—again, but knew nothing could stop this now. He fingered the trigger, forcing the muzzle to bear on Mitch, and found himself thinking: *I wish I knew which of them killed Dad.*

The gun bucked against him, only half raised to his shoulder. From a corner of his eye he saw the hammer leave Dan's hand. He had no time for movement, other than a brief head movement, and the short-handled hammer gave his temple a grazing blow, one that had no force to stun, but that took a square inch of skin from his head.

He swung the carbine to cover Dan, having no time to look at Mitch, and momentarily he expected the slam of a bullet, the brief pain and the oblivion that would follow. Dan's carbine lay a yard before him on the ground, and the man threw his body toward it, missed his first grasp, and clawed frantically. Burt shouted: "Dan, I'll kill you!"

A shot roared; a bullet showered Burt with splinters. Dan

would not stop trying, and Burt dropped the rifle muzzle and fired. Dan jerked, found the carbine, but seemed unable to raise it. Burt looked for the source of the shot, saw Mitch lying on the ground, revolver wavering wildly in his hand.

Sim panicked, and flung both handfuls of dynamite sticks at Burt. A couple of them hit him, having no more hurting power than potatoes, and the rest thumped harmlessly against the rock floor.

Movement and action had backed Burt into the main tunnel, and suddenly he turned and ran. Another handful of dynamite sticks came after him, landing on head and shoulders, and then he was out of range, swallowed in complete darkness.

His lungs strained to bursting. The only sound here was the pound of his feet and the tortured gasp of his breathing. He heard talk, shouting, the beat of hoofs, and stopped, terror-stricken until he thought: *The Riorsons are still behind me.*

Then he began to shout. The wild shaking of reaction trembled in his limbs, and sobs tore at his throat. This was the way John Cross found him.

The tunnel is sealed now. Cattle roam the Clear Creek Valley, sleek and fat, and Stella Norden, now Stella Cross, is serene and happy at Clevis Cross. There is a new house in Nordens' meadow, for Lucy's and Burt's family is increasing.

Yet there are other times, when dust clouds sweep across the meadow, that Burt will remember, will think of the three Riorsons behind the gray walls of the state's prison. There are times when he will think of Mitch, dead on the gallows for the murder of Nick Norden. He will finger the long knife scar on his thigh, and then he will smile—for all that is past. He will smile a deeper smile for all good things that are yet to come.

About the Author

Lewis B. Patten wrote more than ninety Western novels in thirty years, and three of them won Spur Awards from the Western Writers of America, and the author received the Golden Saddleman Award. Indeed, this points up the most remarkable aspect of his work: not that there is so much of it, but that so much of it is so fine. Patten was born in Denver, Colorado, and served in the U.S. Navy, 1933–1937. He was educated at the University of Denver during the war years and became an auditor for the Colorado Department of Revenue during the 1940s. It was in this period that he began contributing significantly to Western pulp magazines, fiction that was from the beginning fresh and unique and revealed Patten's lifelong concern with the sociological and psychological affects of group psychology on the frontier. He became a professional writer at the time of his first novel, MASSACRE AT WHITE RIVER (1952). The dominant theme in much of his fiction is the notion of justice, and its opposite, injustice. In his first novel it has to do with exploitation of the Ute Indians, but as he matured as a writer he explored this theme with significant and poignant detail in small towns throughout the early West. Crimes, such as rape or lynching, are often at the center of his stories. When the values embodied in these small towns are examined closely, they are found to be wanting. Conformity is always easier than taking a stand. Yet, in Patten's view of the American West, there is usually a man or a woman who refuses to conform. Among his finest titles, always a difficult choice, are surely DEATH OF A GUNFIGHTER (1968), A DEATH IN INDIAN WELLS (1970), and THE LAW AT COTTONWOOD (1978). No less noteworthy are his previous **Five Star Westerns**, TINCUP IN THE STORM COUNTRY, TRAIL TO VICKSBURG, DEATH RIDES THE DENVER STAGE, and THE WOMAN AT OX-BOW. His next **Five Star Western** will be BLOOD ON THE GRASS.